CHILD OF THE SEA

By Ines Khai

ISBN-13: 9798373943949

Cover art by: Andreyaa Hora
Logos and cover layout by: Eno Krüger
Library of Congress Control Number: 2018675309
Printed in the United States of America

For Kimya, Rosita, Ines, Manvie, Léonie and the countless

women who came before us.

Thank you for inspiring me everyday.

For Mawsi Khai, thank you for always believing in me.

Once upon a time, a little girl called Maya was born in a village near the sea. She took her first breath and started crying. She cried when she was cold. She cried when she was hungry, when she needed to be changed, when she was tired. She cried when no-one could guess what she needed. She even cried in her sleep!

Her mother was so exhausted that one night she stood up, and started rocking baby Maya while walking around the house with her eyes still closed. She had been taking care of these night tears for a few months now. With her eyes closed, she opened the door and walked down to the sea. She didn't really know what she was doing. She simply felt called to bring her crying baby to the sea.

When she saw the waves and smelled the salt, Maya's mother started crying too. Oh, how she hated the sea! This violent force who took her husband, leaving her alone to deal with a sad baby who would not stop crying. « *My poor baby must be crying for her father to come back.* » thought Maya's mother, as she stepped onto the wet sand. « *Maybe that's him calling me to present his daughter to his new home under the sea.* »

Before she knew what she was doing, her feet started moving faster towards the sea and she could feel the waves dancing around her ankles, her knees, her thighs, her waist. She was moving her arms up and down to bounce her baby in and out of the water. Each time she brought her back up, she heard an unusual and delightful sound: laughter. Her baby was laughing. « *Is that what you needed all along?* » She asked.

« *All this time, what you needed was the sea. All these tears to feel the salty water on your skin. You don't have to cry anymore. All you need is here.* »

They danced in the waves all night, until the sun was ready to rise and the first fishermen noticed them on their way to start their day.

Aren't you Ida? The wife of our late neighbour? What are you doing here, at this time, and with your baby? Shouldn't you both be sleeping at home?

She didn't say anything. She knew they would not understand. She knew anyone spotted doing anything unusual was in danger of being called crazy or worst, possessed. She felt they had likely already made up their minds regarding her sanity. She was tired and worried they might call somebody else to witness her behaviour and comment on what should be done about it. She weakly waved and turned around to walk back to her house.

As soon as she was out of the water, her baby started crying again, but this time, it was a different cry, a silent one. Tears were rolling down her cheeks but she was smiling. Her eyes were saying « *Thank you Mama, thank you.* »

A couple of hours later, when the sun was high in the sky, Ida heard someone knocking at her door. When she opened it, she recognised her neighbours. All the ladies who lived nearby, bringing coffee, cakes and worried looks.

What is this that we heard? You were in the sea with baby Maya before the sun was up? Why? What were you doing there? You would never hurt your baby, right? We know she cries a lot but...

Their eyes were now open wide with anxiety. They were looking at each other with silent questions for a while, until one of them finally said:

Ida, where is your baby? How come we don't hear her cry?

Ida calmly walked to the bedroom and came back with her baby.

See? There she is, and she is crying. Quietly. Crying quietly, that's all. The sea made her feel better.

The neighbours were speechless for a moment, taking turns to have a closer look at Maya and her never-ending fountain of tears, and yes, these were quiet tears. They were amazed, but still worried. They left the coffee and cakes on the table and quickly excused themselves.

When she looked at the window, Ida saw them talking to each other, making large hand gestures, shaking their heads and shrugging their shoulders dramatically. When they noticed her watching them, they waived and walked away.

Ida never got any visit from her neighbours again. None of them ever stopped to talk to her like they used to do when they saw each other in the village streets. Now they crossed the street or entered a shop before she could even say hello. The fishermen never commented nor greeted her again when they saw her and her baby dancing in the waves at any time of the day or night.

Weeks, months and years went by without any friend. Ida thought about moving back home, but her mother was so far away, on another island and up in the mountain, away from the sea, which was not an option for Maya.

She remembered leaving her mother with mixed feelings after meeting her husband. Relief and guilt; relief because she had never felt this life was for her. Working hard in the garden to sell fruits in the market, long hours and just enough money to survive. She wanted more, so when the nice looking and soft-spoken man told her about his travels on the sea and his beautiful village on the beach, she packed her two dresses and said goodbye. She felt relieved, her new life was about to begin.

But she felt guilty. What kind of daughter leaves her blind mother to her hard life like that? It had always been just the two of them, living alone in this little house in the mountain and cultivating fruits her mother sold at the market once a week. Her mother used to say:

My sight is not good but I am doing alright.

As a child, Ida used to believe it was just that. Not such great sight, which is a slight inconvenience, but nothing major. It took growing up and hearing other people talk about her mother to realise she was actually blind. She liked staying in her house and her garden because she knew every corner like the back of her hand. She needed no help to go from one corner to the other and do whatever she needed. She didn't need any help to go down to the village and sell her produce because she had grown up doing this with her mother. People in the village used to say:

Seeing her walk like that, you'd almost forget she is blind!

Still, she had always felt her mother needed her help. She was always volunteering to go with her every time she needed to leave the house and she was telling her about any obstacle on the road. When she met the sweet talking man, she repeated to herself everything her mother used to say and everything people in the village liked to say. She convinced herself her mother would be alright by herself and she had a right to live her own life. She repeated this to herself many times but deep down, it didn't feel right. She left and felt that, because of her heartlessness, something terrible would happen. She would be punished. Something would certainly happen. It was a matter of time; she could feel it. But nothing happened at first.

The village was just as beautiful, if not more than what he had promised. His love was all she had ever dreamed of. They got married. He went to the sea for a week or two here and there. His absence was unbearably long every time but he always came back with all sorts of gifts and fancy fabrics that could not be found around the village. Nobody around had dresses as unique as hers. When he was home, it was all long conversations, laughter, dances and love. She was happy, happier than ever.

When she became pregnant, she started worrying again. « *Is this too much?* » she wondered. « *Is this too much happiness for someone like me?* » She touched her belly all day and all night, praying for a healthy baby and a safe delivery. The morning when she gave birth, the sun was about to come up when she felt the first pains, but the sky was grey. There was a storm outside and the sea was angry. Her neighbours came to check if she was ok. They found her on the floor, contorting with pain. She gave birth in a matter of minutes, with the support of her neighbours. The baby started crying and the neighbours' husbands came in. Back from fishing early because of the storm. Back with bad news because of the storm. Back because of the sea who took her husband, leaving only parts of his boat scattered around to give clues about what had happened. She would never see him again. Never hear his voice. Never dance with him. Never watch him sleep. Never wonder « *Is this too much happiness for someone like me?* »

Four years have gone by now. She can barely believe it when she looks at her now walking and talking daughter. She is still crying, but just one tear here and there now. They had gone to multiple doctors and specialists over the years. The doctors had prescribed eye drops and glasses, which only made her eyes turn red and her head hurt. They had performed all kinds of tests and exams, which all turned out to be useless. They couldn't find anything wrong and had no explanation for Maya's condition. They promised they would be in contact soon after researching more and discussing everything with their colleagues, but Ida never heard back. After too many disappointments, she had stopped looking for more doctors and continued going to the sea.

After her husband's savings were gone, Ida had to find a way to earn a living. She had to face the fact that her only work experience was in her mother's garden. Then she fell in love and let a man take care of all her needs. She couldn't do that again. She was done falling in love so she turned down any man who promised to take care of her despite her crying baby. Even the courageous ones who didn't care about her reputation and talked about love, she had to turn them down too. They pretended to love her, but they always had to mention the tears and the sea. They were asking for the sea baths to stop. They wanted a sweet and normal life. They did not want any crying baby nor any wife who walks to the sea at dawn. They didn't want her really, because of who she was: a woman who walks to the sea with her crying baby. Anyway, none of them could compare to the love of her life. Not even close. They would all end up adding their voices to the voices talking about her in the village. She had become the talk of the town, and not in a good way. She had become a pariah and soon, there were no courageous men knocking at her door anymore. So when the money from the savings was gone, she thought she and her child would starve. She thought she would just lie down in bed and wait for death to reunite her with her love.

2

Until one night, she was laying awake in bed, staring at the ceiling and worrying about finding food for breakfast. She had taken mangoes from a neighbour's tree last week and was not proud of it. She had made peace with her status at the village. She was a pariah. Yes, that's what she was. That's what they were, her and her daughter. She was fine with being a pariah, but a thief? Is that what she was becoming? Could she be ok with being a thief? Certainly not. It was causing her sleepless nights over a few mangoes. Once! It was just once.She thought to herself: « *I took some mangoes... no, say it! Say it, Ida, Say it! It was theft!* » She whispered: « *I did it. I stole. I stole some mangoes. I am a thief.* » She held her head into her hands and tried breathing slowly to stop the tears. « *A thief! I am a thief!* » Breathing in, breathing out, trying to ignore the inside voice that kept screaming « *Thief! Thief! Thief!* »

She felt a little hand on her shoulder.

Mama, my eyes hurt!

Maya's eyes tend to be dry at night. The only thing that helps is to pour sea water in them. Ida grabs the bottle on her night stand but it is empty. How could she let this happen? She usually always makes sure she has some sea water at home in case Maya needs it, but on this night, the bottle was empty. All these money problems distracted her and now Maya was suffering.

Come one baby, let's go for a swim!

As always, Maya ran out immediately. Ida never had to tell her twice. Just mention going to the sea and she was out the door.

Ida smiled. It takes so little to make Maya happy. All the stares in the street, the whispers around them and the frugal plates at every meal could never spoil her happiness as long as she could jump into the sea and laugh in the waves. She was jumping and swimming and waving at her mother, disappearing under the waves and jumping back up again. Again and again.

Ida sat there, on the wet sand, smiling, thinking « *Maybe it takes little to make me happy too. She smiles, I am happy.* » Maya ran back to her mother with her two hands cupped and a bright smile.

Mommy, look what what I have found! It's so pretty!

Ida looked and could not believe her eyes. It was a pearl! And a big one!

Where did you find this? she asked.

In the sea, over there! Maya vaguely pointed at the sea. *I felt it under my foot. I thought it was a rock but it is too pretty to be just a rock. It's for you Mama, do you like it?*

I love it!

Another sleepless night. Ida is looking at Maya, listening to her light breathing, smiling at her little peaceful face and holding the pearl in her hand. She could sell it, but how would she explain where she found it? Would she be accused of being a thief? Where would she sell it anyway? There was no jewellery shop in the village. People had to go to the city when they wanted to buy a gold chain or a ring, and who knew if this kind of shop also bought pearls? Who could she ask? There was no one she could talk to. She couldn't just walk up to someone who had been ignoring her for 4 years and ask them for advice about where to sell a pearl that mysteriously appeared out of the blue, but what was the alternative? Hours of walking with a toddler and getting into the first shop to ask if they wanted to buy a pearl?

When she finally woke up, it was extremely hot, the sun blazing, sharing more heat than anyone could handle. It was this moment around noon when everyone was looking for the cool shade of a tree and the breeze coming from the sea. This was no time for laying in bed with all windows closed. The house was quiet, too quiet. Ida suddenly got scared and jumped out of bed quickly, calling:

Maya? Maya!

No answer. *Why was it so quiet*? Ida checked every room and was opening the windows as she went along. She could feel the breeze on her skin but she was still hot, and now sweating. Where was Maya? She opened the back door and looked at the little path that lead to the beach, and there she was, walking back home with a bottle full of sea water. Ida could not believe what she was seeing. Her four-year-old child went to the sea by herself to fill out her sea water bottle. The feeling of guilt swept over her. That same old feeling of guilt. She had become way too familiar with it over the last few years. Guilt for not liking farm work and dreaming of a different life. Guilt for leaving her parents. Guilt for not finding how to fully cure her daughter's eyes. Guilt for going to the sea under everyone's disapproving gaze. Guilt for being a pariah and making her child a pariah too. Guilt for still grieving after four years. Guilt for not knowing what to do to earn a living now. Guilt for considering selling the pearl her daughter gave to her as a gift. Guilt for those mangoes. Guilt for forgetting to fill out the sea water bottle last night. Guilt for sleeping while her daughter went outside all by herself. She sat on the floor and hugged Maya when she reached her. Maya's left hand was closed behind her back.

What's in your hand, Maya?

Slowly, Maya opened her hand and revealed two beautiful pearls.

She said you should sell them. Maya said.

Who said that? Who gave you that?

My friend in the sea. She called me and gave me the pearls. She said there are many more and you should sell them.

Can I meet your friend?

She is always there in the sea but you never see her.

Let's go, I want to have a better look. Maybe I will see her today.

They walked to the sea and, instead of sitting on the sand as she usually did, Ida walked in the waves with Maya in her arms, like the very first time. Then Maya started swimming and playing. She was laughing, giggling as if she was with someone else who was tickling her and saying something funny.

Ida had never noticed this before. All the times she sat on the sand, watching from afar, lost in her own thoughts, she had never noticed that the way Maya played in the sea looked like she was not alone there. But now she noticed it looked like she was playing with someone. Ida tried focusing and squinting her eyes, trying her best to see but she couldn't see anything. Just Maya, having a good time with who seemed to be an imaginary friend. But the pearls were real. These were not imaginary pearls. They were real and they could solve the money problems Ida was having. She was wondering how much she could get for the three pearls when Maya swam back to her and gave her four more pearls.

Can you see her?

No baby, I can't see her. It looks like you have a special friend that's only for you. Go say thank you, we have to go now.

3

Movement. Action. She felt this was what she needed now.

No overthinking, no calculating, only action. She walked back

home, Maya's little hand in her right hand, the pearls in her

left. Going, walking, actions, nothing but actions. No thinking.

Rinsing the salt from their bodies.

Getting dressed in their best clothes.

Combing their hair neatly.

Filling a bag with a small bottle of water, another one of sea

water and the seven pearls.

Closing the house and walking. One foot in front of the other.

Again and again until they reached the city.

It was a good thing that Maya was a quiet child. She could

remain silent for a long time and this was what she was doing

there. No complaining about the long walk, no questions

asked and this was good because Ida could not answer any

question. She didn't really know what she was going to do

once she reached the city, where she was going to go, and

she did not want to think about it. She didn't want to think, at all. She was focusing on the one action she needed to perform at this time. Walking away from the guilt. Walking away from the shame, from constant worry, from sadness and grief. Just walking. With every step, she was feeling a little bit lighter, so she kept going forward. One step after the other.

On the way back home, Ida was feeling anxious, looking all around her, checking behind her shoulder to see if anyone was following her or would jump out from behind a tree. She wondered if she looked as suspicious as she felt. It didn't feel right. Her purse felt heavy. There were several notes in it. She knew notes, even several of them, were light but still, her purse felt heavy. She had never had that kind of money before. Her husband had. He had always brought back what she felt was a lot of money every time he came back from his travels. He used to go from island to island, buying from one to sell to the other and then coming back home with gifts and money to add to the saving box. He used to say it was the family's savings but she always thought of it as his money. She had never had any money for herself. His money was not her money. She had not earned it. Even after he was gone and she had to use the money to survive, she would still think of it as his money. It was to feed and clothe his child, but it was for her too, and she was feeling kind of guilty about it. She knew he'd want her to use the money but still, she felt it did not belong to her and she didn't like spending it, but she did spend it. All of it. Slowly. A piece of bread here. Some clothes when Maya got bigger there. Surely. All the little things added up. She was reasonable and never got anything they did not absolutely need but you couldn't make one note last forever. She slowly and surely spent all the money she had not earned, and now here she was, walking around with money in her purse. She accepted that although she had not earned this money either at least it did not belong to anyone else. For a moment she considered that it was Maya's money. But Maya was only four. Then she remembered: « *She said you can sell them.* » The pearls were a gift from the sea given to her via Maya. Given to her with permission to sell them. There has been no instruction to give the money back to the water. Just « *you can sell them.* » So she did sell them and now she had this money and she felt the money belonged to her. When she got out of the shop, she walked to the market and bought a huge sandwich to share with Maya. It was full of marinated vegetables and aromatic sauce. She also got some coconut water and after some hesitation, a big slice of cake. She sat on a bench and shared the feast with Maya.

The sun was going down when they started making their way home. Maya was sleepy from the long walk and the excitement of the city. Being tiny, Ida did not struggle too much carrying her on her back most of the way home. What made the journey difficult was the anxiety that came with walking at night with money in her purse. She was worried about being robbed or just interrogated. How would she explain being out in the streets with a child at this time? How would she explain the money in her purse? Her heart was beating hard and she was sweating, praying for the journey to be over soon. Again she tried to calm her thoughts and focus on her body. She smiled when she reached the village and then her house. She got Maya into her bed and went to the bathroom for a shower. Feeling calm and refreshed, she counted the money and placed it in the saving box. She checked on Maya, who was fast asleep, then quickly walked to the sea by herself. She sat on the wet sand and cried in silence; for once, those were not tears of despair nor shame. It was pure gratitude. She let the waves caress her feet for a moment and whispered.

Thank you. Thank you. Thank you.

Walking back, she felt like she was hearing the sea for the very first time. It was like a song with rich harmonies and a steady rhythm. It was beautiful. She had been so focused on herself that she had never taken the time to listen. All this time, she had been clearly missing out. She stopped to listen more carefully, closed her eyes and swayed to the rhythm, for how long? She didn't know. For as long as it took her mind to go back to Maya and she hurried back home to check on her. She was still asleep, poor baby. That was a lot of walking for such a young child. She had been a real little soldier. No complaint, no question asked, only silence and trustful companionship. Ida checked on the saving box again and then fell into a deep sleep.

« *Was it all a dream?* » That was the question on Ida's mind when she woke up, well rested, with thoughts of pearls and money in her saving box. It all felt like a dream. Pearls gifted by the sea. It felt unreal, but there was nothing unreal about the soreness in her legs. She was not used to walking that much. She had never been to the city before. She had never needed to. She could get everything she needed for everyday life at the village's market and her husband used to bring back from his travels anything else she could dream of, so why bother going all the way to the city where it is noisy and dangerous? Her husband used to tell stories about the great dangers he had to face in the cities. Every island had their great cities and what they had in common was too many people, including thieves and murderers. She liked the stories but also found them terrifying. She trusted her husband was strong and smart but who knows with all these dangerous people? Anything could happen. She prayed for his safety every time he had to go, and she simply stayed away from the city, convincing herself she was content with her village life.Even as a pariah, she felt she was safer there than anywhere else.

She had thought about leaving many times since he was gone, even more since she had become invisible, but where would she go? Wouldn't it be the same anywhere else? She would still be a sad widow who brings her child to the sea at any time of the day and night. She would always be suspiciously strange. So she stayed. This was the place where she had a house. She thought about selling it but she couldn't bring herself to do it. She felt she had to stay. Now she was thinking about the pearls. Had she sold the house and walked away, she wouldn't have received this gift. It still felt like a dream so she moved her legs to feel the soreness. was real. She grabbed the saving box and counted the money. Real.

She heard the familiar steps in the corridor and soon Maya was in her arms.

Mama, can we have cake for breakfast?

She smiled. Maya was right. They had been struggling for a long time and were now in a better place. They could treat themselves.

Yes, we absolutely can. Come on, let's get ready to go out.

They walked the village's streets with large smiles on their faces. The same people who usually ignored them were now looking at them with questions in their eyes. They were so used to seeing sadness and shame on Ida's face that today's joy felt out of place. They did not understand it and didn't like it. More disapproving looks. Ida didn't care. She felt lucky, happy and hungry. She entered a shop where she had not set foot since last time her husband came back to the village, more than four years ago. He used to take her there to buy her the sweetest and prettiest cake. It was their celebration ritual every time he came back from a long travel. She had not been there since, even when she still had money left from the saving box. It didn't feel right to go without him. It didn't feel right to experience anything sweet, have any joy without him. She had not even missed the pastries. She was too overwhelmed with grief, but today she wanted to remember the sweet memories. She wanted to create new sweet memories with Maya, so she got into the shop, picked two pretty cakes, smiled and presented some money to the cashier.

The news flew around the village like it was delivered by telepathy. It went up and down every street, slid under closed doors and made its way through open windows. It reached every living soul and whispered in every ear.

Ida doesn't seem to be broke anymore. She was seen smiling and buying cake. She was seen going to, then coming back from the city and now she is buying cake.

Ida knew that rumours would start, that people would wonder why she suddenly had money to spend on cake. She knew someone must have spotted her on her way to or from the city. She knew that everyone would get she got some money there in a suspicious way, but she didn't care. She was enjoying some cake with her smiling daughter, they would then go get some clothes as well as some groceries. She would get everything she wanted and let whispers sing all around the village. She had another song to listen to. Even away from the beach, she could now hear the sound of the waves dancing and twirling and kissing the sand. It brought her peace. She felt like everything was fine. The only slight disturbance was the soreness in her legs.

After leaving her groceries at home, she took Maya's hand and walked to the beach. She walked into the sea, letting the waves massage her legs. She stayed there until sun down. She spotted eyes with looks that wondered if she would stay there all night with her little child. Even on this sweet day, the looks were still stinging so she decided to go home to get away from them. « *I guess I still care a bit what people think* » she thought as she walked back to her purse on the sand. The moon was far from being full and nobody could see her in the dark evening. She grabbed the extra slice of cake she had bought to take away and cut it in two. She gave a piece to Maya and said:

Give it to your friend.

Maya ran back to the sea with her offering. Ida took the remaining piece of cake and walked back into the sea. She placed it gently on the surface and tried to see how it moved down and away with the movement of the waves. She whispered:

I don't know why you are helping me but I want you to know that I am grateful. I don't know if that's the right way to thank you. I will do differently if you let me know how.

She closed her eyes and listened. The whooshing sound of the see was strong and harmonious. It made her feel safe and blessed.

For the first time in years, she felt everything was ok. She felt she and Maya would be alright. She felt it and she wore the feeling on her face, on her body, in the way she walked, the way she moved. She always seemed to be moving to a rhythm, almost dancing. She was smiling and swaying, like there was some music in her ears. A melody that made her smile.

There was just as much going to and coming from the sea. There were more trips to the city and more cake eating, more smiling, more staring when she walked down the village's streets to buy whatever she wanted, more questions in the air, more guesses, more bets. Everybody wanted to know. How come Ida was all of the sudden able to go and buy all she wanted? Where did the money come from? From the city of course. It came from the city. No need to be a genius to guess that. Many people had seen her going to and coming from the city. She started going there and then became a regular at the cake shop. Nobody had ever seen her lift a finger but now her bag was full of money. How do you earn any money when you are a lazy woman? She was never a hard working woman. She showed up one day, married to the village's most eligible bachelor, making all the young women around jealous. Sure, she was beautiful but there were plenty of beautiful women around here too. Why did he go who knows where to find her and put her in his house near the sea? A house so many local girls could see themselves in. He was always charming to them, smiling to whoever waved at him when he was back from his travels, telling stories about what he had seen abroad, showing the fabrics, jewels and delicacies he would sell to big shops in the city, giving them huge discounts when they really liked a fancy mirror or a shiny necklace. They liked to bring him food. Isn't that the way to a man's heart? They brought him delicious meals and he always complimented them on their cooking skills. They let him know about any party organised nearby but he never invited them. He never wanted to go. He always had something to say about how shy he was in big crowds, how he needed quiet time when he was home after his adventures, how he had to get ready for his next trip. And off he went, smiling and waving at whoever was on his way to the sea. Some got discouraged and married someone else. Someone less exciting, less rich but someone who wanted them. Someone who was not away on the sea most of the time. Someone who could not make them dream with stories of colourful adventures but who would hold them at night when the wind was yelling and the rain pounding. They married that someone else and sometimes they looked at the sea, wondering what their life could have been if they had waited and found the dish that was the actual way to the traveller's heart. Others had tried harder. They did not marry anyone else. They said no to anyone who tried. They said no and improved their cooking skills. They became more adventurous with their use of spices. They talked to elders about old traditional recipes. They discussed moon rituals for confidence and manifestation. They decided to be patient. They kept up with the latest fashion trends and turned on the charm to the highest level. All of that without success. They tried so many things but the only thing that seemed to excite him was to go back to the sea. After a few days in his house, he always started talking about where he wanted to go next, what he thought he could buy, who he knew would want the items and the long silent moments on the sea. He would talk about the water like it was a woman, the perfume of it, the shape of its waves, the sound of her voice, the colour of her skin. He had to go back to her.

Those who married someone else whispered between themselves, swearing that the man was in love with the sea and no woman would ever have his heart. Those who were still hoping thought one day he would get tired of the cold blue water and would need a warm body to hold. All of them thought it did not make sense for a man his age, not an old man but no longer a young man, to be alone and not want to start a family. So they should not have been surprised the day he came home with a shy woman and said he had just married her. Was it not what a man his age was supposed to do? Get married? Yes, it was time but why go outside the village. They thought he had disrespected the village women, equally beautiful as the stranger he brought back as his wife –

and unlike what they would later realise, much more hard-working. They had spoiled him and now he was being ungrateful, bringing a stranger here. Feelings were hurt but it was a village of proud and polite people so Ida was welcomed and eventually made to feel at home. When they got to know her, people were pleased about how polite and helpful she was. Jealousy and bitterness disappeared. She became part of the village. Neighbours visited when he was out on his travels. She was supported during her pregnancy. But then he disappeared for good – claimed by the sea, his ultimate woman and wife

And then the baby cried all day, all night without interruption. And then she started going to the sea with the baby at all hours of day and night. It looked like Ida could not help it, like she was hypnotised by the waves. Her body could not resist the call of the sea. Just like her husband before her and everybody knew how it ended for him. Now she and her baby too seemed to need the sea way too much. Everybody was looking and thinking about how this could end. And what could you do to stop tragedy when the main antagonist is a powerful element like the sea? All you can do is hope you don't catch the curse. Stay away, let the story unfold away from you and the ones you love, because what you see when watching from afar looks way too much like a curse and who likes to be around cursed people?

Nobody was proud about the way the whole village had abandoned Ida and her crying baby.

They could see Ida walking around with sadness in her eyes, how hurt she looked at first when she greeted people in the streets and nobody responded. Then how she turned silent, how empty her eyes became. She would enter the shop, show some bread to the cashier, place some money near the register and leave in silence. That was the only thing she came to do. Always very early, when the shop was not very busy yet. She would spend the rest of her time in the house or in the sea. Some were worried she might kill herself or the baby. Grief made people do terrible things. Others thought it was the sea that would do something. Maybe swallow them and never let them out, like it did with the traveller; or take them away and have them appear on another island, like the traveller had mysteriously appeared here one day. So they would keep an eye on her if they happened to be around during one of her worrying sea baths. They would watch and count how many seconds she held the baby under the water. She'd always bring the child back up for air. They'd be reassured enough to leave but not enough to think she was sane or safe.

They'd think it all made sense now. The traveller came out from the sea one day with enough money to buy a nice house near the beach. He was coming and going with his boat, selling and buying, getting richer and richer, surrounded with the village's finest women and picking none of them. Most men resented him for making it hard for them. How do you compete with him? What stories do you tell? Not everyone had travelled so much nor could show fancy items from abroad. However, they could not help but liking him once they got to know him. He was good company. Men liked his stories and jokes too. When he came back married to this girl from the other side of the island, they secretly made fun of the local girls who had turned them down, hoping to catch his heart. They would have to consider them now. Maybe they would be the ones playing hard to get now. The girl got pregnant, the traveller kept on travelling, village women started going out with village men. Everything was going well, until the storm. Until they found crushed parts of his boat on the same day when the child was born. A baby girl. A healthy baby but nobody could say if she was cute because her face was always distorted with who knows what feeling. Was it sadness, anger, frustration? Was it hunger, some kind of discomfort or physical pain? Nobody knew why but the baby was always crying. The women had gone to Ida one by one to try and find a solution, a remedy. They had been singing every song, holding the baby in every position, massaging her, bathing her with every herb, rocking her, dancing with her, praying. Nothing had worked. Everybody pitied Ida, the poor woman was exhausted. The pain of losing her husband and the lack of rest with her crying baby. It was more than most could handle. So when she was spotted in the sea with the baby before sunrise, it was difficult not to get bad ideas about her intentions. What a relief it was when the women confirmed the baby was well and alive! What a surprise it had been to hear that the baby was now crying quietly. Not a sound coming out of her mouth.

The sea took her father away.

And it was the sea that took her crying away.

It had always felt like the traveller had a special relationship with the sea, like it had blessed him. Maybe the women were right. Maybe he really was in love with the sea before he met Ida. Maybe the sea was in love with him too and decided she didn't want to share him with a woman. Maybe the sea wanted the baby too, forcing Ida to bring the child to her at all times of day and night. Maybe... A lot of maybes stirred among the villagers. Not one of them with a good ending and nobody wanted any part of it, so everybody stepped away, pretending to ignore them but secretly watching from afar. Because everybody wanted to know whose guess was correct. In all the maybes, all the guesses, nobody had come up with any possibility of Ida suddenly having money to buy cake. Ida walking around with a smile on her face, like the sea was not after her and her baby. Ida looking blessed rather than cursed. It was confusing and they did not like it. Somebody had to do something about it. It was way too unnerving not to know what was going on. Everybody wanted to know.

4

The looks grew more intense. The whispers became louder.
The mystery was too much to handle and there was no hiding
anymore, no more discrete commenting. Ida could hear
everything and see familiar faces on her way to the sea, on
the road to the city. She started fearing the day when
someone would come to her and ask « *where does your
money come from? Why are you suddenly rich? Are you doing
anything illegal? Should we get the police involved?* » The old
questions she had asked herself before were coming back to
her. « *is this too much happiness for me? Is something bad
going to happen?* » She was not as happy as when her
husband was still there. She still missed him. The nights were
still extremely lonely but, at least, there were no money
worries and it was a huge relief. She was able to take good
care of herself and her baby. Maya was happy, she was
happy, so the old feeling came back. She remembered her
mother and the way she cried when she left. She cried and
said she'd miss her for the rest of her life. It was five years

ago. At first, Ida had not even thought about visiting. She was too busy living the good life in her beautiful house. Then she thought about it after Maya was born and her traveller gone but he was the one who had brought her here on his boat. She'd have to pay a lot of money to travel with someone else, and she needed to be careful with her money, to make it last. She thought about it some more the lonelier she got but the money was disappearing a little more every day.

Now she had some money. The feeling was back. Was that too much happiness for the ungrateful daughter? But now the daughter was able to visit, maybe even stay. She was thinking about it but a symphony of what ifs was playing in her head and it was loud. What if her mother was upset with her and refused to see her? What if she had moved and she couldn't find her? What if she was dead? Every island had its fair share of storms every year, and it had been five years. A few souls aways decide to travel with the wind of the storm. A few souls always decide to travel any day any time. Every moment was time to go for someone somewhere. She was thinking about it, visiting, but all these questions paralysed her. Every time the thoughts got too loud, she walked to the sea and listened to the sound of the waves. She relaxed and let her mind go blue, calm. She walked in the water and floated for a moment. No more questions in her mind. Only the sound of the water and Maya's laugh.

She was taking more and more of these baths and she was whispering to the sea, talking about her worries and asking for a sign. She was letting the waves rock her softly until she felt sleepy and called Maya to get back home and rest. She started having vivid dreams about home. She could see her mother. She was never talking to her in these dreams, just standing there, looking at her in silence. The look in her eyes was different in every dream but it was always very intense. Not eyes vaguely directed in her direction and half closed, but open wide and fixed on her, starring right into her soul. The look was loving sometimes, sad other times. It could be angry too. Every single time she fell asleep, it was the same dream. Her mother, standing in front of her house, staring at her with one of these looks. Her eyes healthy, staring into her soul. Ida had come to fear falling asleep, as she knew the dreams would come, and with them, the guilt. The guilt was growing and becoming unbearable. She had to go home. She had to go and tell her mother she had not forgotten about her. She had to introduce her to her granddaughter. She had to share her luck so her mother could live more comfortably. She had to tell her the story of Maya and the sea. She had to risk her mother thinking she was cursed.

She made up her mind in the middle of the night, waking up in a sweat from a dream with her mother's angry eyes. She was right to be angry. Too much time had passed. She had to go home and apologise. Now that her decision was made she couldn't sleep. She started packing. Not much, just a couple of dresses for herself, not many more for Maya. She grabbed a couple of nice fabrics and jewels left from the old times. She couldn't go home empty handed after all this time and she thought there would be no time for gift shopping in the morning. She would leave before sun up and walk to the city. She should be able to find a boat sailing home or at least some information about the next one at the harbour. Her plan was made and her suitcase packed but it was still too early to leave and Maya was fast asleep. She was still feeling energised, excited about the trip ahead. She walked to the sea and left some flowers for the waves. She gave thanks for the dreams and sat in silence for a while, feeling she had made the right decision.

It was still night when she went back home to wake Maya up and get her ready to go.

Why are we leaving so early? She asked when Ida told her about her travel plans.

Because there is an early boat we should take to see the sunrise on the sea. How beautiful do you think this will be?

It will be so beautiful! Hurry Mama, I don't want to miss it!

She felt bad about lying to Maya but she needed to get her excited about the trip too. Truth was she did not want to see anyone on her way and she had no clue whether there was an early boat going to her home island or not. All she knew was that the looks and the whispers had recently become more difficult to bear and some people had been walking behind her when she had tried going to the city to sell her pearls. She had changed her mind and gone back home a couple of times. She did not want to deal with people investigating to find out what she was doing. She did not want to explain where the pearls were coming from. She did not want to explain where she was going now, even when she was simply going to visit her mother. She was getting tired of all the attention and almost missed the old days when she was invisible. So that's how she wanted to leave, discreetly, like she was invisible. She did not want anyone to notice. No explanation. As she was walking, she surprised herself wondering if she would even come back. She had taken all the pearls and all the pearl money with her. She had taken Maya's bottles of sea water, their favourite dresses and her late husband's favourite shirt, which she still wore sometimes when she felt lonely at night. What else would she ever need?

Anything else was dispensable. She could live without it. Anyone could break into the house and take everything inside for all she cared. Was this house ever a home after he left? All these thoughts were rushing into her mind while she was walking. It was still dark but she could see the lights of the city. Almost there.

Is the sun coming up soon, Mama? Will we to get to the boat on time? Maya asked.

I think we have time. We are almost there.

When they reached the harbour, there were only workers there. People carrying merchandise to huge boats and fishermen getting ready for the day. They were welcomed by surprised looks. It was not common to see a lady and her little daughter dressed in their Sunday bests in the harbour that early in the morning.

Ladies, do you need any help? Someone asked. It was a tall man with an amused look on his face. Maya got scared and grabbed her mother's leg.

We are looking for a boat to travel home, ideally today.

Well, you are way too early. Only merchandise boats and fishermen leave that early. You'll have to wait at least 2 or 3 hours for a tourist boat. You see that building over there? Come back later and they'll tell you if there are any tickets left for where you want to go.

But we want to see the sunrise on the sea! Said Maya.

You can watch it from the coast, young lady! Unless you want to come catch some fish with me! Hahahaha!

He turned his back and walked away, still laughing. Ida looked at him until he disappeared behind a building. She waited for a while, thinking he might come back. She had felt safe in the presence of this stranger. She wished he would come back. Maya pulled on her dress and Ida smiled at her.

Let's go.

They walked up to the building the fisherman mentioned and saw the timetables and ticket prices. She had more than enough money for their tickets and she had two full hours before the office opened, as well as two additional hours before the first boat to her home island leaved. She took Maya's hand and walked back to the bench where they sat on the first day they came to the city together.

We will watch the sunrise from there, She said.

They sat and quietly watched the sky changing colours as the sun rose. They watched the city wake up and the first street vendors get ready for the day. They had breakfast on the bench in front of the sea and got their tickets when the office opened. With the two hours left, they went to the jewellery shop to sell the pearls, bought more gifts at the market and

daydreamed about home.

5

All these years, she had felt like she was so far away from home but only a couple of hours and there she was, recognising the harbour, the city centre with its street vendors and colourful shops, the music in the air, the joyful conversations. She was home. Almost. Her steps took her to the same old place where she found the same old bus with red writings on the side. She embarked with Maya and started feeling nervous. In an hour or so, she'd be so close to her mother's house. She'd have only a couple of hours walk to get to the little house up in the mountain; the little house where was had grown up and from where she had run away five years ago, thinking she would never come back. She couldn't decide what she would say exactly when she'd see her mother again after all this time. She started rehearsing in her mind but everything she could come up with felt wrong. How could anything feel right? There was no right thing to say. She tried calming herself by closing her eyes and breathing deeply but the apprehension was growing bigger and bigger the closer they were getting to home. So when she finally reached the little flower garden in front of the house, she froze. She felt like her heart was about to explode. Maya was looking at her with questions about to burst out but she could not move a muscle. She could not go to the door and knock. She could not say a word. She wanted to run but she could not move. Until Maya let her hand go and started waving at someone who was standing at the window.

She will not wave back Maya. Did you forget? I told you her eyes are not great, ok?

Ok, but can we go now?

Sure baby, let's go.

They knocked and when the door opened, Ida couldn't speak but her mother immediately said:

Ida, is that you?

Yes, it's me, Mama. It's me and my daughter Maya.

I thought you would come. I've been having those dreams. I knew you would come. Come in, come in.

She held Ida tight a for minute and then turned to Maya:

Maya, you come sit with me and tell me everything about yourself.

Maya took her hand and sat with her and talked for hours. Ida had never heard her talk that much. She described their house, their village and the sea with details Ida would never have thought to mention. She described the people too; people Ida never knew Maya had ever noticed. She gave their names and occupations as well as pretty good impersonations. Then she said who was the meanest and who looked sad when they passed them by. Finally Maya talked about the pearls and trips to the city. She talked about the cake they ate now that they had money. Ida didn't try to stop her. She was too busy watching her mother's face to try and guess if she was worried or scared but all she could see was pure joy. It was the face of a woman who was meeting her granddaughter for the first time and enjoying the company of a funny and chatty little one. She did not show any concern, even when Maya mentioned her friend in the sea and how her eyes hurt if not washed in sea water. All she said was:

Oh… really… your friend sounds nice…

When Maya told her about giving cake to her friend, she said:

All that talking about cake is making me hungry! Have you had lunch yet?

When Maya replied no, she stood up and said:

Let's go to the kitchen and prepare something. Do you know how to prepare some food Maya?

No. Mama prepares food for me.

Then come on, Maya's mama, come help me.

As Ida entered the kitchen, she was pleased, if not surprised to see that everything still looked the same. Everything was at the same place and she sat at the table like she used to. She grabbed the knife she used to use and put her hand out so her mother can pass her the fruits. It had always been her task to peel and cut the fruits. She remembered the exact size her mother liked them so she peeled and cut until her mother stopped handing fruits. Then she stayed there, watching her work and looking at Maya, who was taking her new role very seriously. Her grandmother had put her in charge of handing her spices. She was calling.

Give me the cinnamon... yes, this one. Thank you, baby. Give me the vanilla, you know the vanilla, right?

The kitchen was filled with a delicious scent from the tea and the fruit salad. Ida could feel herself salivating. She knew how to prepare a fruitarian meal from seeing her mother do it for many years but she had not been preparing any at all since she had left. She never had the patience to peel and cut that many fruits and add the spices, pick the right herbs to make some tea. She used to find it so boring and weird. She knew no one who ate like that. Her mother had an aversion that salt that she never explained to anyone. To anyone who asked, she simply replied that she had a sweet tooth and Mother Nature always provided with no extra cooking needed.

When Ida moved away, she used to buy meals from street vendors most of the time and her traveller was not difficult. He didn't expect her to be a perfect housewife. He didn't care about her not knowing how to cook. He loved her not her cooking skills. Now she was back home and smelling her mother's usual meal. She had not been bored helping her prepare the fruits. She realised she had missed these moments and maybe she had not been preparing any meal because it had felt wrong to be in the kitchen alone. Now her

heart was light and content. She realised it was not the being

alone in a kitchen but the being away that had felt wrong.

Now she felt things were right, she was home.

6

Leona hadn't cried in such a long time it took her a minute to understand why her face was wet. She brushed a tear away and licked her finger to taste the longtime lost but oh so familiar salt that she had avoided all these years. She remembered her mother screaming:

Why are you crying so much? Why do you cry all the time? Do you enjoy crying? Is that what's happening here? Did I give birth to a crazy child who enjoys crying?

The truth was that she did. She enjoyed crying. It made her eyes feel good, her fingers too when she rubbed her eyes. It made her whole body feel good. Her eyesight had never been great, but as a child, when she cried for a long time, she could see better. Everything was better. She wanted to cry all the time just to feel better. She never had to force it because, when she stopped even for a few minutes, she was missing the salty water so much it hurt. Her mother didn't seem to understand. Nobody did. As soon as she was able to accept that nobody got it and ever would, she taught herself how to cry in silence, how to escape adults and even children's eyes so she could cry quietly alone and feel better for a while. As soon as she could walk, she'd step aside and wait until no-one was looking at her to let a few tears get her eyes wet and maybe roll down her cheeks. She shivered and smiled. These quiet crying moments were what she was looking forward to when she was acting all day, pretending to be who everyone wanted her to be. A normal child, a smiling child, a playing and laughing child. She pretended to be all that as long as she could have her quiet time here and there. As long as she could dream about leaving one day and living a life where she could cry where and when she liked without anyone having any comment to share about it. Hiding behind a tree, she would cry and smile.

She got caught many times and got mocked by children her age, interrogated by adults, screamed at by her mother. She was not allowed to cry; she was not allowed to feel better.

She should be happy and smile. Smile when her eyes hurt, when her skin was so dry it cracked. She tried for a while to spend more time at the river. The water made her feel ok but something was missing. It did not feel as good as tears. She heard about the sea. She heard the sea was salty water, just like tears and she wondered how good it would feel to bathe in water that felt like tears. She sat at the market, listening to merchants talking about sailing to distant islands on their boats. They talked about the sea that smelled and tasted like salt and she wondered how it would feel to just dive into the salty water. She asked her mother if women could be sailors too and Freda laughed. It was so rare to see her laugh. She was beautiful when she did, but on that day, Leona did not want to marvel at her mother's beauty. She wanted an answer to her question. She wanted a positive answer. She wanted to know that one day, when she grew up, she could be a sailor and friend to the sea. She could hop on a boat, pretending she liked to transport people and merchandise from an island to the other and, at night, when everyone would be asleep, jump into the water and feel the salt on her lips. Her mother laughed and called her ridiculous. She told her she should give up these silly dreams, that the sea was not for her. The sea was cursed and would destroy her if she ever went close to it. She said she had made a very conscious decision to stay away from the sea when she came to live in this village, far away in the mountain and it was the best decision of her life. She said her silly father decided to stay close to the sea and he was dead now. The sea had killed him. It was what the sea did, killing people. The sea would kill her like she had killed her father if she ever went to her. Is that what she wanted? To die and to break her mama's heart? Is that what she really wanted? It was not a rhetorical question. Freda was watching her straight in the eyes, waiting for an answer.

No mama, that's not what I want.

Good, then you stay here, keep on growing the fruits with this green thumb of yours. Make some money at the market like me and live a good life away from the sea. That's what you are going to do. Get these silly ideas about the sea out of your

mind. The sea is not for you!

The words hurt and her dream became dry and cracked like her skin. She sat in silence until Freda finished selling all her produce and talking to all her friends. Then they walked home in silence. Leona didn't say a word when Freda rubbed her skin with vaseline and complained about it still being so dry. She waited for total silence to make sure she was alone to cry without being caught. She did it as a habit, like she did every night, without thinking about it, but that night was different. There were no tears on that night. No tears on the following night. She had cried so many times for so many years and now it felt like she could not cry anymore. She remembered her mother coldly stating so many times:

If you keep on crying like that, w*hen I die, you will have no tears left for me.*

Her mother was well and alive but she really had no tears left in her. There was no hope left in her. The sea was a distant dream she could never reach. She did not want to keep on dreaming about the sea and being faced with disappointment everyday until the end of her life. She was banishing every thought of the sea from her mind. She was banishing the sea from her being. The salt, she was banishing it from her life. She stopped crying and her sight declined even more. By the time she was 16, she could not see anymore. She had always lived in the same house, gone to the same garden and market so she was able to go from one place to the other without any difficulty. She was walking confidently, eyes half closed with an indifferent expression on her face. Freda took her to hospitals that smelled odious with sickness and disinfectant, to houses that smelled of herbs and strong teas. They gave her pills to swallow with her meals, teas to drink and concoctions to place on her eyes but nothing worked and she did not care. Freda seemed more upset than Leona was about her own fate. Leona did not care about seeing. She had no desire to see nor to do anything really. All she wanted was to be left alone so she did whatever her mother told her to do. She went to the garden, went to the market, cleaned. Freda forbid her to cook, fearing any accident with fire. Leona stopped eating cooked foods and turned to fruits, nuts and seeds. Freda thought it was a temporary reaction to not being allowed to cook and let it slide, thinking it would pass. But it didn't. It was the salt. No more salt in her life, no more tasting it, no more thinking about it, no more dreaming about the sea. She had started to live a new life with no hope of ever feeling better.

After a year of not seeing and not talking, one morning Freda woke her up before sunrise and told her to get ready to go. For the very first time in a year, Leona felt the urge to speak. She had questions. Get ready to go where? Why so early? To do what? She opened her mouth and closed it. She was trying hard to kill the beginning of hope she had started feeling when her mother told her she had to go. She did not want to get her hopes up and be disappointed. She was now afraid of asking any questions, of asking the question that immediately came to her mind. The sea, are we going to the sea, is this where we are going? Freda looked like she had just read her mind.

I said get ready to go. You are going, I am not going anywhere. I have work to do here. Do you think this garden is going to take care of itself? We can't both travel at the same time. You are going alone. Listen to me, and get dressed while I explain. You will walk down to the market place. Then, you will walk to our usual spot in the market. From there, you'll go left and find a large road. You'll go down this road for around an hour, until you find a crossroad. Someone will wait for you there and you will follow her. That's all you need to know. Take this bag, there is some food and a bit of money in it.

Freda looked at her daughter for a while and said:

I am sorry. I lied to you about the sea. I wanted to keep you for myself. I should have told you the truth and seen if you'd want to stay with me anyway. Now you go down there and see for yourself. I hope you'll come back.

Leona looked at her mother. She had a lot of questions but Freda was a "because I said so" type of woman and everybody knew not talk back when she had given her orders. She had a big heart, Freda, always sharing whatever she had with whoever needed it. Always giving advice to whoever asked, listening to every broken heart, filling every empty pocket. But she was also the type of person who liked things done a certain way. She had that look that made you weak. She was a strong woman. Many men were intimidated but many more tried their luck. None of them ever knew her touch. There had been some talk at first, when she arrived to the village with her round belly and started growing fruits for a living. She made friends easily but never told her story. Nobody ever learnt about the baby's father nor any family member.

I came here to start a new life. I don't want to talk about the past. I left it behind for a reason.

That's the most anyone ever got from her. She was a mystery, Freda. No-one fully understood her. No-one, not even her daughter.

Leona had dreamed of going away but not of never coming back. There was always some coming back in her dreams of escape. Becoming a sailor, swimming in water that felt like tears but returning home all the time. Going on adventures, feeling great in the water and coming back. That was the plan when she still had dreams. Thinking about never coming back was scary.

Go now, hurry up. It's safer with no-one around.

A quick hug and a pat of the back. That's all she got from her mother, who thought she might never see her again. Leona was confused and scared but she wouldn't dare question her mother so she obeyed, like she always did. There was no excessive thinking involved. She was simply executing orders. Her mother knew best, she had to follow orders. That was and had always been the only option.

She walked to the market, turned right, walked down the largest road for a long time and grabbed the arm of the lady who was waiting for her. She introduced herself as her mother's old friend and said they should hurry before anyone saw them. She took a breath and said « yes », pushed the word out with effort. First time talking in more than a year, her voice sounded like the voice of a stranger. She decided silent Leona was someone from the past. She was someone who had no hope for a better life. No hope for the sea. She was here for the sea so there was some hope. There was a reason to speak. Surely, this lady would explain what her mother meant by the truth and why she had been sent here. She started formulating a first question in her mind when she realised her mother's friend was already walking away. She had to walk faster to grab her arm again. They walked quickly, as if someone was following them but Leona could not hear any steps nor noise behind them. After a while, she smelled an unusual scent and she knew immediately what or who it was. The salty scent. She had never smelled it but she recognised it. It was the sea. She did not realise she was walking faster and faster. She had let go of the lady's arm. The woman caught her arm back to try and slow her down, without success.

Slow down young girl, you're going to trip! I'm going to fall!

But she could not hear her, all she could hear was the sound of the waves, the steady rhythm of the waves going back and forth. She let go of her arm again and let the sound guide her in the right direction. When her feet reached the sand, she stopped and took her shoes off. She opened her arms wide, turning left and right to look for her walking companion, but she could not find her.

Don't worry, I am here. I just don't feel like getting my feet wet. Go ahead, I know you want to go.

Her mother's words came back to her.

The sea will kill you like it killed your father… I lied about the sea… I should have told you the truth…

The confusion, the fear, the attraction to the sea. She wanted to jump into it and, all at the same time, she felt like she could not move. She started with one little step, then another one, and one more, one more. Until her feet got wet, until a wave tickled her toes and that was it. She took her dress off and ran towards the sound of the waves. She jumped into the sea like she had dreamed of doing for so many years. She let the waves rock her slowly and all her worries disappeared. She felt just like she had imagined all these years before, when she was dreaming in the river. She felt at peace. Her skin was not itchy, her mouth was not dry and her eyes. She opened her eyes under the water. The dull ache in her eyes was gone.

It was simply no longer there. She felt good. Her whole body felt amazing. She turned over and floated, eyes closed, smile wide. Bliss.

Hey! Come back now, that's enough for today!

She opened her eyes and saw that the sky was changing its colour. The sun was not far away, the morning would be here very soon. It felt so natural to see, she was not even shocked. She simply opened her eyes and saw the sky. She looked at her mother's friend. She was waving her arms frantically and gesturing for her to come back. She did not want to go back but she actually wanted to talk now, more than ever. She wanted to ask questions, many questions, so she waved back and started swimming back to the beach. She had not realised she had been drifting so far away. She had learned to swim in the river as a child but she had never swam any long distance. There was not enough room in the river for that. Now there was a decent distance to swim before she could reach the beach but she was not worried about it. She was comfortable. She could move easily in the sea and go where she wanted without much effort. It felt as if the waves were reading her mind and transporting her. Her feet met the sand and she grabbed her dress.

Come on, fishermen will be there soon. We don't want to meet anyone. Hurry!

They were walking fast, almost running. Leona was breathing hard. Talking was not an option. She was focusing on following the surprisingly fast woman. When they finally reached her house, the woman pushed Leona inside and closed the door. The sun was slowly coming up outside but it was dark inside with only a few rays from the street lights coming though the shutters. Leona sat on the floor to catch her breath.

My name is Lola. The woman started.

She left the room and came back with a pitcher of coconut water and a plate full of fruits. She placed them on the table and pushed a chair for Leona.

Sit here. Eat.

She lit a candle. Leona realised she was starving and really thirsty too. She started eating and drinking while keeping an eye on Lola, who was now sitting in front of her and smiling.

You look like her. The exact same face. When you got out of that bus, I couldn't believe my eyes. I was walking fast because I wanted you to see the beach before anyone could ask what we were doing there, but I was also very confused and almost scared. It felt like I had a ghost walking behind me. You look just like her.

Like who?

Ah yes, you talk. She didn't talk, so there is a difference. Your mother told me you had stopped talking.

I had, but I guess now I have started again.

Good, that will make things easier.

What things? I don't understand.

Freda did not explain?

No, she said I should go and see for myself. I don't know what she was talking about. Something about the sea.

Yes, you saw the sea alright. And she saw you too. You were drifting so far away. At some point, I wondered if you were ever going to come back. That's what happened with her you know. First she stopped seeing, then talking. And one day, she went to the sea. She drifted away and never came back. I was there. I saw it happen. I saw it with my own eyes.

We all saw it.

Who? Who drifted away?

Freda's mother. Your grandmother. You didn't know that?

My mother never talks about her life. I know nothing.

Nothing? Really?

I know my father was killed by the sea.

Well, that's a way to put it. If you want my opinion, he could have easily avoided it. The sea is not something to mess with. A man is only a man, no match for the sea. Anyway, we never knew where nor how she met him. Maybe he knew how to sail or thought he was a good swimmer, that would explain why he thought he could just jump into the sea and fight strong currents.

What would she say when you ask?

She wouldn't answer. She was very secretive you know.

And you never insisted?

Of course, I did but there is no getting any information from her unless she is well and ready to share. She's calling the shots, always.

I know.

There was silence for a while and Leona looked around. It was a simple room, clean, all blue and white with big shells on the floor. Lola stood up and opened all the shutters. Then she unlocked the French windows and used the shells to keep them wide open. The sun was coming up now. The two women sat in front of the window and looked at the sea, breathing in the salty air.

What now? Leona asked. *What am I supposed to do? What am I supposed to see for myself?*

I am not sure myself. I guess you're supposed to go to the sea, just like you did earlier.
What happened back there?

I don't know. Nothing. I was just swimming, that's all.

Swimming that's all? Really? Nothing happened with your eyes? They didn't look like that when I met you up there.

Do you think my mom knew the sea water would cure my eyes?

Of course she knew. Why else would she send you here?

Is it a special beach? Do people come here to be cured?

No, there is nothing special about this beach. No-one has ever been cured of anything here. That's just you. That's just you and maybe your grandma. Freda's mom. She was just the opposite of you. In the sea all the time and perfect voice, perfect vision. Once she stopped going to the sea, no voice and no eyes. One day, she went back to the sea to never be seen again. That was years and years ago. So long ago, yet people here still talk about it.

Lola looked kind of sad all of the sudden. Her eyes fixed on the sea. She looked like she was done talking. Leona wanted to be polite and patient but at some point she couldn't take it anymore. She needed to know. Maybe that was why she was there, to know more about her family history. Maybe that would help her understand her mother's decision to go up to the mountain and never come back. Maybe she had some family members around here. Maybe… Her mind was racing. She really needed to know more.

Ms. Lola, please. Will you tell me what happened?

Lola looked at her and said:

"I will tell you everything I know."

She went to the kitchen to make some tea. She came back, gave Leona a cup, took a sip of hers and started talking.

7

I was born here. My whole family was born here. I never went anywhere and never want to go anywhere. Look at this, she said, pointing at the window, *there is nothing more I want to see. People from here, we all love the sea. We are sailors and fishermen, teaching our children about the sea so they can keep our traditions. It's only recently that our children have started going away, turning their backs on our way of life. I haven't seen my children in years. They went so far away.*

Anyway, I grew up here, in this very house, and look over there, she pointed at an old abandoned house across the street, *that's where your mama grew up.*
One day, when I was 5 years old, I was playing outside and I saw a little girl my age I had never seen before. It was your mama, she had just moved in with her mom and she was looking at me. I waved. She waved back and that was it. We became best friends.

Her mother had arrived one morning and asked if there was

any house she could buy. She was told about this house

across the street and she bought it immediately. Got some

money out of her bag and bought a house. Nobody had ever

seen that before. A woman with enough money in her bag to

buy a house. And there was more. She was walking around

buying things and nobody knew where her money was

coming from. People tried becoming friends with her so they

could ask questions and understand what was going on but

she was very shy and, when people knocked at the door, she

would say she had a headache and needed to rest. Men tried

courting her so they could share her wealth and also

understand where it came from but she used to say she had a

broken heart and could not love anymore. She was a mystery

and everybody loves solving mysteries. People started spying

on her. They started noticing that she was taking night sea

baths. They started thinking it was very strange, suspicious

really. They also noticed she was not going to church like

everyone else. They wondered whether she was worshipping

the sea. We do love the sea here but we don't bath at night and become mysteriously rich.

People started noticing that she was waking up very early to go to the city sometimes, taking your mother with her. They wondered if she was making money during these trips to the city and how. They started having bad ideas about how she might be making her money. Was it unchristian rituals and unchristian encounters? Everybody had their theories, none of them good. At some point, people stopped trying to be friends. They simply stopped talking at all. They started avoiding her. My parents even told me I could not play with your mother anymore.

I was sad and even angry, but I was a child. There was nothing I could do. I would sit here and look at the window. I would see your mother sitting alone across the street. Some children would sometimes say mean things to her as they walked by and there was nothing I could do.

Sila, she was called Sila, your grandma. She stopped taking night sea baths. She stopped going to the sea at all.

Everybody knew because there was always someone keeping

an eye on her. So she stopped the sea baths and she also stopped going to the city. She started growing all kinds of fruits and going to the market to sell them. She could grow good fruits, really sweet ones. Everybody thought she was doing a good job. Eventually, people started talking to her again, but she was done talking. She was wearing a sad face and looked like she was just too tired to talk. She was smiling sadly and shaking her head yes or no. That's all the response anyone could get out of her. She started getting sick. It was her eyes, always wet, always crying. She was not crying like she was hurt or sad. It was more like her eyes were leaking. She cried and cried and cried like that for years. Everybody tried helping. Some brought her herbs to put on her eyes while she slept at night. Some prayed over her. Some tried convincing her to go and see doctors and healers. She did not seem too convinced but she went anyway. Unfortunately, there was no good result. Her eyes kept leaking all day all night. It lasted such a long time, until one day, out of the blue, it stopped. Her eyes were dry but she could not see. She could not see anything. When it happened, your mother was

16. She took over part of the gardening and the selling at the market. Her mother always by her side, sighing and nodding like it was a secret language only Leona could understand. Your mother was the only person who could communicate with her. She was the centre of her life. It made your mom feel special sometimes but frustrated most of the time. She felt like she could not go outside and live her young woman's life, in case your mother would need her. She wanted to do what we were all doing it. Sit on the beach and talk about boys, pretending to ignore them when they walked by and at the same time, hope the ones we liked would invite us to the next party. There was always a party, always new dance moves we were practicing and we were eager to show off our skills at the first occasion. Freda would spend a little time with us, learn half the dance and make her excuses so she could go home early and see if her mother was ok. She'd tell everyone that it was fine, that she was happy with the way things were but we all knew she was lying. I tried talking to her about it. I had been allowed to be her friend again when her mother had stopped all the sea and city business. We were very close but

she was getting very quiet and refusing to answer anytime I

tried to talk about her mother's health and why she was doing

so great when she first arrived. There was a secret there but

she was not ready to share it yet. Sometimes, I could see her,

sitting outside her house, looking at the sea for hours. I

wondered what she was thinking about. I would cross the

street and sit next to her, telling her about what she missed at

the last party, showing her new steps in case she'd want to

come next time. I'd always say she should try to come but

she'd never came. The years went by and everybody in our

group age was getting married. I got married myself and

became pregnant. She said « you're so lucky you don't have

to worry about any curse for your children. » I asked why she

was saying that and what curse she was talking about but she

said she had said too much already and should go and see if

her mother was ok. She went home and didn't get out for

days. When I saw her a week later at the market, she said she

had felt unwell and did not remember much about that day.

As always, I understood that it was her way to say she could

never elaborate on what she had told me. It had been like that for years. We would have a good time, really great conversation, then she would say something cryptic and refuse to explain. Anytime I would insist to know more, she'd cut me out. Use her mother as an excuse to go home and not come back. Sometimes, I'd get upset about it and ignore her too, give her taste of her medicine. But I'd always go back to her. I don't know what it was about her. I suppose it was because one day, when I was five, I had decided she was my friend and I had never been able to go back on that. So months went by and I had my baby, my first son. He was perfect, so beautiful and full of energy. Your mother was great with him. She was always offering to babysit and she really was a natural. He loved her so much. She told me many times that she wanted a child, that she felt she could risk it. I knew better than to ask about the curse so I said nothing. I only said « you know you need a man for that, right? You're going to find one while sitting in your house with your mother every night! » She smiled and said « maybe I have already found one. » I asked questions and she did not answer. She never said who it was but made it clear she was in love. I tried *keeping an eye on her to see if I could catch her going out to*

meet anyone but I was busy with my baby and my husband. I

did not really have time to play detective. She never

mentioned the guy again, until I noticed that her belly was

growing rounder. She smiled and confirmed she was

pregnant. She worried about telling her mother. She said she

had promised not to have any children. She kept on going to

the garden and to the market. People congratulating her on

her pregnancy. She was the kind of pregnant woman

everybody wants to be, no morning sickness, no aching back

and a glowing skin. No-one could help smiling when they saw

her. Everybody was smiling, but Sila who was clearly upset.

Still silent but you could read the anger, the disappointment

on her face. One day, a nice looking man stopped by their

market stall with flowers and presented them to Sila.

Everybody knew him. He had a fancy flower shop. Rich

people came from all over the island to get them from him. He

had no family and was always bragging to anyone who asked

about the fact that he would one day have a huge family, at

least seven children. He said he was in love with Freda and wanted to marry her. He said he was proud to be the father of her future child and wanted to start a big and happy family with her. All the nearby merchants and customers had stopped their selling and buying so they could witness this lovely moment. Everybody was smiling and clapping but to their surprise, Sila stood up and threw the flowers on the floor. She stepped on them and started crying. It was not the old leaking of the eyes we had witnessed years before, it was more, so much more, an unreal amount of water coming out her eyes. The water flowed down her face, her clothes and to the floor. It looked like she could see again. She could see through the fountain of tears. She looked at her daughter with sadness, shook her head and walked away. Without a word, she simply walked away. At first, nobody moved nor said anything. The amount of water coming out her eyes was surreal, the shock got us all paralysed. The first one to move was the florist. He said « I'll talk to her. » and ran after her. He was trying to reason with her but she was walking faster and faster. He was young and healthy but he was struggling to keep up. At this point, we were all running after them because we could not believe what we had just seen, we needed to take a better look. She was rushing towards the sea. When she reached the beach, she started running and there was no stopping her, she was so fast! She jumped into the water and floated away. Just like that, she floated away. Your mother's guy jumped into the water too. Your mom screamed « Don't go! It's dangerous! ». He screamed back « I'll get her back, don't worry! » But Sila was only a small dot, far away near the horizon line now. Was it pride, bravery or plain stupidity that made him feel there was nothing supernatural going on there and that he was strong enough to retrieve her? I don't know what it was but the florist kept on swimming, even when we could not see any trace of Sila anymore. He swam, stopped for air, swam again, stopped, tried again. At some point, he tried coming back. Some guys from the village hopped on a bark and went to his rescue. They did as fast as they could but they reached him too late. What they came back with was not the man your mother loved, it was only a body. Freda laid on the sand and cried loudly. We tried calming her down, without success. When we helped her stand up to leave, she got away from us and ran towards the sea. She beat the waves and screamed. We had to almost fight her to get her out of the water. We took her to my house so she could grieve and rest until her baby was born. That baby was you. We were waiting for you to be born, but instead of resting and grieving, your mother quickly went back to the garden and the market. Working was all she did. Working and barely spending any money. I should have guessed she was saving. Every time I mentioned maybe meeting someone else in the future, she rejected the idea and said her heart was broken forever. She said Sila had warned her. She said she could not live that close to the sea anymore, that it was a painful reminder of what had happened. I asked « What happened? Where did your mother go?». She said « She went back. » Then she pretended to be tired and went home for the night. I promised myself I would ask again in the morning and find out about the curse and all the secrets she had been keeping for me all these years. I swore to myself that I would not back up. Maybe it was something I could help with. If it was really a curse, maybe I could look for someone who might help. We all *know there are people with gifts who can help with these situations. I went to bed with all these thoughts on my mind but when I woke up, I felt sick. I was pregnant again and just as sick as the first time; Not everyone gets to have a perfect pregnancy. Because I was unwell, I did not go to Freda first thing in the morning. I felt better only later that day and I went to meet her at the market, but her stall was empty. Nobody had seen her that morning. I went to her house and she was not there. The shutters were closed and remained closed all day, all night and the day after, and the week after, and the month after. She was gone. She had left me without saying goodbye. I was so angry. What kind of friend does that?! I thought maybe we were actually never friends. Maybe I was only the silly girl who was the only one willing to put up with her secrecy. I felt like I had never known her and never would.*

A couple of years went by and one day, I received a letter from her. She said she was sorry about leaving the way she did but she could not take it anymore. The sound of the waves, the smell of the sea, the blue sea everywhere around.

She had moved to the mountain so she could not smell nor hear it, only see it maybe sometimes but at least from afar.

8

She said a long time ago, a woman was made captive to come work here for free. She was traveling on the ocean with fellow unlucky captives. She came from a family of griots and had already begun following in her ancestors' steps, so she sang to her companions to give them hope. She sang about soldiers who won many wars. She sang about healers who cured many pains. She sang about happiness to provide sweet dreams. She sang loudly so all could hear. She sang so loudly the captors asked for silence. They asked for silence and her people asked for more songs so she sang some more. She got beaten and sang through the pain. She got gagged and she hummed through it. She got choked and, while she suffocated, she clapped the rhythm of the song her people liked the most. Her body was thrown into the ocean and sank down to the bottom of it.

The last piece of her life still in her body pushed her to clap again this rhythm that was like the beat of her heart. She clapped and clapped. She clapped and the water danced.

The Spirit of the water enjoyed the rhythm so much she decided to bring the griot back to life. She breathed life back into her body and changed her so she could be able to live in the water. It was somewhere in the middle of the ocean with no land around. Nothing but the cooler blue all around. Blue life.

When the griot realised she had not died, she rejoiced. She started singing songs of thanks. She was so grateful she sang for days, weeks or months. She didn't know how long she sang these songs of thanks. She was so happy to have been saved. She thought she could sing these songs for all eternity. The griot had lived her life to delight people with her music. She had done it under the sun, she could do it under the water now. She decided this should be her new life. She clapped and sang for the spirit of the water and her kingdom. She clapped and sang for weddings, births and many happy occasions but there was no wedding for her, no baby and no celebration. Spirit had made her able to live in the water and be like water natives but she was still different. She was self conscious of her appearance, which was still human when *everyone else was more like water. They all fit the sea so well*

and she stood out. At some point, her body started changing,

becoming more like water but the process was very slow. She

didn't know how long it would take for her change to be fully

completed. She didn't know how long she had been there.

There was no way to know how much time was passing. She

started feeling unhappy about her difference. She wanted to

be like everyone else at first but after a while she started

remembering her old life. Her life on firm ground. Walking on

firm ground, looking at the sky. It was so far away down the

sea, the light of the sun was a far memory. How the griot

missed the sun!

She started singing about the sun. She sang about the light,

the warmth and the colour of her skin. She missed the deep

brown of her skin. In the time she had spent underwater, she

had witnessed her skin changing, the colour disappearing,

until she became almost as translucent as Spirit and her

people. At first, her eye could not distinguish them from the

water and she kept running into them. Now, her vision was

perfect and she could see every movement in the sea, she

could see everyone with her accustomed eyes. She could see that she was becoming one of them. It seemed to be taking very long but she was getting there and she didn't like it. She was grateful for still being alive. She had been miraculously saved. She was grateful… or was she? She felt that maybe she was only trying to convince herself. Anytime she had a moment to herself, she was remembering her life before the sea, before the boat. She remembered her family, her friends, life under the sun. She remembered the moon and the stars. And the wind, she remembered the wind. She remembered fruits and vegetables, sauces. Drums, she remembered the drummer she loved and her dreams of having children. She looked at her life and saw that it was comfortable but it was not really her life. She had been saved from a life of captivity but she was now a different kind of captive. She wanted out. She wanted the sun, the moon and the stars, the wind on her brown skin. She sat at the bottom of the sea and sang « Spirit of the Water, o! Manman Dlo, I have sung for you, I sing for you, I will sing for you. Spirit of the Water, o! Manman Dlo, I will sing for you even if I am far away. I will sing for you even if

I walk under the sun. I will sing for you even if I dance on the ground. I will sing for you everywhere I go. » The song went on and on for days, maybe weeks, maybe months. There was no way to be sure. She stopped to eat or to sleep but any other moment was for singing this song. She sang and sang. She sang until Manman Dlo came to her and said:

So you want to go back up there?

The griot nodded yes.

I have listened to your song and it pleased me, but will you keep your promise? Will you remember me and sing for me sometime?

I will. I will sing everyday. Now that I know that this song pleases you, this is the one I will sing first, everyday. I will teach the song to my children so they can sing to you everyday too.

That's an even bigger commitment. Every day? And are you sure you want to make this decision for your children? Maybe they won't want to sing.

They will. I am so grateful for you saving me. It is my pleasure to sing for you and they will sing too.

I will take you up so you can walk the earth. I will provide for you so you never go without but you gave me your word, so you must keep your promise.

Again, the griot nodded yes.

You know I had to change you so you could stay here. Children were not part of the plan, but I see you really want children. You will have one. Your child will have a life like the one you had before because I know this is what you want deep down; but your child's child will have to sing because you want to include your descendants in your promise. If she doesn't, I will stop providing but her body will crave the sea.

The same will happen to you if you stop singing for me. This will go on for the generations to come. Do you agree with this?

The griot took a moment to think about it. She could have a happy baby who will live to experience the sun, the moon and the stars. Then, she could teach her grand-baby songs to please Manman Dlo and the grand-baby can sing to her. Or, she could ask her child to never have any children. She nodded yes.

The griot was transported up to the surface. Waves carried her to the beach on a nearby island. She found herself clothed, with her pockets full of pearls.

9

Lola stopped to look at Leona.

Leona, you're crying. Are you ok? Is the story upsetting you?
You can stop for now and continue tomorrow. Anyway, I have
to get to work now. Do you want to wait for me here or come
along? It's at the beach, you could go for a swim if you like.

The story was not upsetting. It was fascinating. Leona loved
it. She couldn't wait to hear more. Of course, she wanted to
go to the beach again and bathe in the sea. She felt like she
needed it. The tears on her skin reminded her of the waves
and the bliss they gave her. She craved it now. She wanted to
go. As they were heading outside, Lola started explaining that
she was working at the beach everyday, preparing meals for
fishermen and it had to be ready for when they came back
from the market, where they went to sell their fish to the
merchants everyday. She was talking in details about the
spices and the cooking methods she was using but Leona

was not listening. She could smell the sea and hear the waves. She was walking faster and faster. She could not help it. Lola was a few steps behind now. She had stopped to greet some people who seemed to be headed the same way. She could hear them speak behind her.

That's Freda's daughter. She lives so far away from the sea. Of course, all she wants to do is to go for a swim.

And you let her go? After what happened to Freda's mother?

She had a quick bath before and nothing happened. I think she'll be ok.

At some point, Lola asked her to say hello. She turned around and waved. Lola's friends waved back and told her to be careful. She nodded yes and walked straight into the waves. When she turned around again, she could see that Lola was gesturing to show where she would be. Leona waved and nodded to reassure her. She didn't feel like floating this time.

She wanted to be fully immersed into the sea. She first floated away and then went down, down until she could touch the sand. She looked around and saw a couple of fishes, some shells and sea moss. She was moving into the sea without swimming really. She was thinking about going left or right or close to that fish. She was just thinking about it and her body was transported there, as if she had been carried by invisible hands. For a while, she was purely in the moment, enjoying the sensations. The water seemed to be lightly hugging her body constantly, making her feel safe and supported. She heard a rhythm and wondered if it was her heart. She heard a melody in her head and remembered the lyrics Lola mentioned in her story. She felt the urge to sing and remembered she was under the water. She suddenly thought about her breathing, the absence of air, and swam back up. When she turned to the beach, she saw that several people were looking in her direction and a silhouette with the same colour of clothes as Leona was waiving frantically so she decided to go back. She moved easily and reached the beach. Leona ran to her.

What happened there? We thought you were gone. You went under for so long!

Really? I don't know, I didn't realise. I was just watching.

Watching what?

I don't know, fishes and shells.

You stayed under the water for a very long time, Leona. I'm almost done working. Are you hungry? I kept you a plate.

I'm sorry, I didn't realise I was staying there too long. Yes, I'm hungry. Thank you.

Lola gave Leona a plate of rice and lentils with fish. Leona had not eaten any cooked food nor animal for a very long time. She remembered when she was still a young child, her mother taught her to eat what she was served so people would not be offended. She looked at the grilled fish in her plate and thought about the fish she twirled around when she had heard the rhythm under the sea. She didn't want to be rude but even the smell was making her loose her appetite.

Is there something wrong with the food? I thought you were hungry.

Yes, I am but I have not really been eating this type of food for so long..

Why? You don't like it?

I stopped eating it when I stopped cooking because I couldn't see and then I got used to eating fruits and salads. I guess I am used to eating like that now.

One of Lola's friends started laughing.

This is the first time someone doesn't want Lola's food and will prefer what I have to offer. It's a miracle!

She looked into a big basket next to her and took out some bananas and guavas. She took the plate out of Leona's hands and gave her some fruits.

There is more in the basket if you want.

She smiled at her friend and gave her the plate. Lola was the best cook around, everybody knew it and she was proud about that. She couldn't believe this child had just turned down her perfectly seasoned food. You could read the disbelief and frustration on her face.

The child likes fruits, get over it! You should be happy she came back from the sea. We all thought she had gone to meet her grand-mother but there she is.

That's fine, said Lola and she laughed, *more for me!*

Lola sat next to Leona and they ate in silence, facing the sea, while everyone else was leaving. After a while, she spoke.

So are you going to tell me where you have been? What or maybe who you have seen?

I was swimming. I don't know, exploring. I was just looking, watching what's down there, in the sea. It felt like I was down there for maybe, I don't know 2-3 minutes.

That was more than 3 minutes, Leona, way more than 3 minutes. We thought you were gone.

Sorry. I didn't mean to worry you.

I know.

Will you tell me what happened next? In the story? So the griot was on an island, with pearls in her pockets. And what happened next?

She met some people who were drumming on the beach and she joined them. She danced and she sang for hours. They enjoyed her dance and songs but they did not understand the words. She had landed somewhere where people spoke a language she did not understand. When the sun came down, they understood she did not know where to go and one of the drummers took her to his mother. She did not want to be a burden so she thought she'd pay for her stay. She gave the woman the pearls she had. When the drummer came back in the morning, the mother showed him the pearls. Both of them tried asking her questions about where the pearls came from but they were still struggling to understand each other so they decided to focus on learning to communicate. At first, with gestures and small words. At this stage, they could already understand each other for basic requests. When the drummer was not around, the mother made it very clear that the pearls had to keep coming if the griot wanted to stay. She was not a mean woman. She was treating her right but she wanted her pearls. She always wanted more pearls. Every time the griot came back to the sea with some pearls, you could see in the mother's eyes that she was already looking forward to the next time. She never kept the pearls in the house for too long. She gave them to her son, the drummer, who was coming back later with money, food and a smile on his face. He was trying to communicate with her too. He was always saying the names of what was around them or what he was giving to her. Pointing and naming: tree, flower, glass, plate. The griot was a fast learner. She quickly became fluent and translated her songs so everyone could understand the words, and everyone enjoyed the songs even more. She was very popular and enjoyed talking to whoever wanted to know more about a song and practise one of her dance steps. She talked a lot about music and dance but she knew she was not allowed to talk about the pearls. It was one of the first things he told her: Pearls, hush, secret. He used to watch her disappear in the waves and wait for her on the beach. When she came back, he always said « It was longer than last time. I thought you were not coming back. » He looked at the pearls, then at her with questions in his eyes but he never asked. He clearly wanted an explanation but was somewhat afraid to know. He didn't know and didn't want anyone to know. The drummer always kept an eye on her, preventing anyone from talking to her for too long. He was always repeating that he wanted to protect her. She thought it was sweet and, after so many years of loneliness in the sea, she let him hug her, kiss her, hold her close at night. She did not know if it was love or only a deep craving for human touch. Maybe it was not love but it was close enough. It was what she had been dreaming of for so long and she wanted it to last for ever.

The years went by and she married the drummer, moved in a nice house with him. He talked more and more about how he needed to protect her, how people wanted to be around her for the wrong reasons, how she needed to make sure no-one found out about their secret. He never liked her going to the sea at night and never really asked how she was getting the pearls. He was of these people who did not want to know. These people who understand but bury the explanation deep down and never want to talk about it. He started going to church more and more and saying that maybe this pearl business should stop. He started getting upset when he found pearls in the house, accusing her of not trusting him to support her. She swore she trusted him and would not bring any pearls anymore. She kept her promise to him. She left the pearls in the sea every time she went to swim and sing. She kept on singing to Manman Dlo every night and let the pearls slip away to the bottom of the sea. Every time she went back home empty handed, he held her close and told her he would always provide for her. He told her the only missing thing would be for her to fully stop going to the sea at night. She said she might stop one day but she never promised.

When her belly started growing, the drummer said it was time to fully stop this sea nonsense. He was worried about this strange behaviour having bad consequences for his child. He always said his child, like it was not going to be her child too.

She worried about that. He said she needed to learn how to be a respectable woman, that a mother cannot walk to the sea at night like a mad person. He insisted on having her word so she gave it to him. She swore she would not go back, and she didn't. At first, she had to catch herself. Her steps were leading her to the sea before she could even think about it. She was catching herself and going back home. He would congratulate her, say:

You see, I knew you could do it, kick that bad habit, I am proud of you.

As the days, weeks, months went by, her vision quickly deteriorated until she could no longer see at all. She became depressed, tired, exhausted. She stayed in bed all day and all night. She could not enjoy anything, not even the blessing of a healthy pregnancy. She spent 9 months laying in bed, crying in silence. At the end of the 9 months, she could not cry anymore. There was not a single tear left in her body. She gave birth to a healthy baby girl and could not speak to give her a name. The drummer named her Freda.

Leona interrupted her:

Freda my mother? Are you saying the griot is my grand-mother?

I am telling you the story the way it was written in the letter I received.

So when the baby was born, the griot kept on grieving her lost sight and voice. She stayed in bed for a full year. She stayed in bed but she took care of the child. The baby stayed in bed for a full year too. The drummer got depressed too and spent more and more time outside the house. He would disappear for days, come back to find his wife and baby still in bed. He would try to reason with her, beg her to stand up and walk to the garden at least.

One day, he lifted her out the bed and dropped her off in the garden, then he sat on the door steps with the baby and observed the griot. She sat there, confused, for a while and mindlessly started pulling weeds. At the end of the day, he lifted her off the ground and took her back home. The following day, he woke up to find her in the garden, collecting fruits from their mango tree. He went out and bought some crops. She instantly knew when and where to plant them. It did not take too long for them to have the most beautiful garden around. They started selling fruits and vegetables at the market. He was playing drums to attract customers while she was dancing with the baby on her back and selling their produce. She was still blind and silent but it was close enough to happiness. Baby Freda was growing healthy and smart, funny too. A happy child. When they were walking near the sea, she would want to go towards the other children who were playing in the waves but the griot would always stop her and the drummer would never discuss it. At four years old, the child had never been into the sea. Not even once. That year, when Freda turned four, hurricane season was terrible. There were storms after storms after hurricane after terrible weather. The sea seemed to want to come up higher and higher to crash everything and everyone. However, it did not crash any house, shop nor anyone. It always came to the griot's house and crashed her garden. People thought there was a message here. The griot knew why this was happening. Deep down, the drummer knew it too. Every time the sea water came crashing against the house's walls, the griot would walk back to avoid it. She did not want a single drop of water to touch her. The drummer protected her the best he could, pushing her to the driest corner of the house and placing himself as a shield in front of the water. It lasted for one, two, three, four, five, six storms, but at the seventh storm, the wood of the wall cracked and a full wave invaded the whole house. The drummer held his daughter close, closing his eyes and holding his breath as the wave went away. When he opened his eyes and saw that Freda was ok, he looked around for the griot. She was not there.

The drummer ran in the night with his child in his arms. As he reached the beach, the storm was over. The sea was calm and beautiful, peaceful. He looked around and, as usual, nothing seemed to have been touched. All his neighbours' houses looked almost fully dry, as if nothing had happened. He looked around. There was no trace of the griot. He walked back to his home and the wall facing the sea had a huge hole in it. The inside of the house was completely soaked. His wife was gone, swallowed by the sea. He walked up and down the wet path the wave had left between his house and the sea. He walked up, stopping and looking behind every tree. He walked down, listening, looking for any usual noise. All he could hear was the soft noise of calm waves. He wanted to scream her name and make her appear magically but deep down he knew she was gone and he knew where. He sat by the sea, so close his feet were wet. With his daughter in his arms, he wept. He was angry. Angry at the sea for taking her but mostly angry at himself for never asking. He knew, of course he knew something special, something magical was going on between the griot and the sea. He knew it from day one. She thought she had approached discreetly and surprised everyone when she arrived that day, but truth was he had seen her. He had seen her come out of the sea. He had seen how confused she looked. Confused and happy. He had watched her hesitate. She didn't know where to go. And then she heard the drums and followed the sound. When he saw her make this decision, he had run to the rehearsal. He was late and they had started without him, so he ran to them and immediately started on a solo. He wanted to impress her. As soon as she reached them, she started dancing and singing. Nobody could understand what she was singing about but she sounded great and was welcome. He wanted to ask her about the sea but she spoke a different language, so he decided to take her to his mother, who was always asking for some help around the house. She reached the house and showed even more magic. Pearls coming from the sea every time she went there, and she went there everyday. She never tried to hide the pearls, she was happy sharing them. His mother became rich, he got his fair share himself and when she started speaking his language, he wanted to ask her about the sea and the pearls, but something was stopping him. Every time he thought about asking her, he became scared about what she *might answer. What if she was some kind of witch? What if she had some kind of evil arrangement? Maybe she could breathe under water and get pearls in exchange of something. In exchange of what? He was too scared to ask. He could imagine, and that's what he was doing. All day, every day, imagining all kinds of things she had to give to the sea. He wondered if his life was in danger sometimes. He wanted to run away from her but he couldn't. She didn't look like a witch. There was nothing evil about her. About the way she talked and moved, about the softness of her skin, the sweetness of her voice. She loved wearing very long skirts and he raised her skirt quickly one day. She thought he was being playful but he was checking really. Nothing wrong with her feet. He was not even relieved. He knew there was something he didn't know and wondered why she was not telling him. She was never willing to talk about her past, where she came from, her family, something, anything. But really, he didn't want her to. He was always telling her that they needed to live in the moment. Enjoy the present and maybe think about the future from time to time but leave the past behind* them. There were some things from his past he didn't want to talk about. Maybe it was fair for her to say nothing if he was going to keep silent. As the years went by, he kept on wondering without asking, shutting down conversations when family or friends became too curious. He then moved to this house near the sea but asked her not to go swim anymore. He had saved enough from all the pearls for them to be comfortable and he was still earning money from the occasional gig and job. He wanted to stop wondering and for her to be normal. He didn't want people whispering around him nor asking him questions about her. He didn't want people wondering where his sudden wealth came from. He was worried about leaving her alone when he had to go sell the pearls. He was worried about her being alone at anytime. He was not entirely sure she would not talk if anyone became too insisting, and if someone had to know, it should be him, not a nosey neighbour. He moved her away from his mother because he came home one day and found her mother interrogating her about the pearls, asking her to get more. He didn't want her mother to exploit her, nor to know more than *he did. And he did not know much. All he knew was this woman came out of the sea, made him become rich and in love. Most people would feel blessed but all he felt was confusion and worry. He understood this was a very uncommon situation, he must have been the one and only man on earth in a relationship with this type of woman and what kind of woman was that? He had no clue. He knew the kind of woman he wanted to be with. Sweet, loving and loyal. This, she already was, but also, he wanted someone who fitted in. Someone he wouldn't have to worry about. This, she was not. He decided he could try to change her. The only issue was the sea thing. If she could stop that, they would be fine. He remembered the day he took her away from his mother's house. His mother screaming:*

She is a witch! You know it! Deep down you know it! I don't know which demon she is lying with in the sea but these pearls do not come for free! Nothing is free, son, you know that! If you marry this witch, you will be cursed! Stay away from her!

He took her to the house he had just bought with the money from the pearls and told her to stop going to the sea. He explained there was no need for pearls anymore. He could work. He could find plenty of work and provide for her. She did not have to go to the sea ever again. She listened and thought about it. She seemed worried, a bit scared. He said he needed her to be the wife he always wanted. She hesitated but in the end she said yes. He felt a huge weight lifted off his chest and started looking for students to make more money. He worked hard as a drummer, a music teacher and any other job that came his way really. He wanted to be happy but he couldn't because she was changing. No more smiling all the time, no more singing. She became silent and she cried a lot. The crying felt abnormal. It was a lot of water coming out of her eyes. It looked like maybe it was an eye disease or something. He took her to doctors and healers but nothing worked. She kept crying and crying until one day she stopped and her sight was gone.

Now he was sitting on the wet sand in the middle of the night with a sleeping child. Maybe he should have listened to his mother and stayed away from this woman. What did he know about taking care of a child? He was not the one staying at home with her all day. He realised he had no clue what they were doing all day. He didn't know how to cook or do anything around the house. He had not spoken to his mother in years. He was too proud to apologise and ask for help. He stood up, walked back to his house, put the child to bed and started on quickly patching up the hole in the wall with what he could find lying around. The wind must have blown his efforts away because when he woke up, his neighbours were watching him from outside, the hole was just as big. It took them all the whole day to fix up the house. They asked questions. All the drummer could say was that the sea had taken her.

He came back to the same place everyday, on the wet sand. He sat there, looking at the waves, waiting for the griot to come back. He remembered the first time he saw her, coming out of the sea, like some come out of their houses. She shook

her head and arms, touched her face, looked at her hands.

She seemed to be surprised about how she looked .

Surprised and happy. She jumped up and down for a while,

hesitated and then followed the sound of the drums. The day

he remembered this, he stood back up and ran back to his

house. He came back with his drum and started playing. He

played for hours. He played until the sun went down and

nothing happened so he went home and slept. He came back

the day after and played again, Freda dancing or napping by

his side. He played everyday. Some days, neighbours would

join him and play in silence. Nobody asked any question. You

don't question how someone grieves. They sat and played

with him until their hands hurt. They shook their heads and left

him so he could play some more. Every night, he would go

home with his sore hands and lay in bed. He'd barely eat what

whoever brought for him and Freda. He'd just lay there,

wondering. What happened? Was she really a witch? Was

there really some kind of arrangement with the sea? Was it all

his fault? He was the one who forbid her to go the sea.

Weren't witches supposed to be evil? She was not evil. Far from it. She was the sweetest woman he had ever met in his life. Every night, he would walk back to the sea while Freda slept and play quietly. He would play this rhythm she taught him, a rhythm that always made her smile, even on her darkest days. This was her favourite rhythm. He played it every night for a full year and one morning, on the anniversary of the storm, she was there. He opened his window and looked at the sea, as he always did. He looked at the sea and saw a familiar silhouette there. She was walking towards the house. It was her. She was soaked. She looked exhausted. It was her.

Lola had been talking for so long the sun was going down now. She stood up and collected her things.

Time to go home!

They agreed Leona would have a last dip in the sea and then meet her at home for the rest of the story. Lola left and Leona laid down under the waves. She stayed there for a while, trying to digest everything Lola had just told her, trying not to think about how long she was staying there without needing to come up for air, trying to stop thinking about the song the griot sang to the sea, trying not to want to sing. It was strange enough that she felt this need to stay under the water like this, she was not about to try singing under water too. There were limits to strange behaviour. She wondered whether Lola was telling the truth or just telling stories. Why would her mother send her to some storyteller? But at the same time, what was going on with the sea? How come she felt so good and could see so well. She opened her mouth and let a long note out. As she did, the water seemed to move around her. She got scared and swam away. She got out and ran to Lola's house. When she knocked, it was not Lola who opened the door. It was Freda. Freda, her mother, was there, looking at her from bottom to top.

10

Freda took Leona's face between her hands and looked her in the eyes.

So you can see! You can see me?

Yes, I can see you. I went for a swim and now my eyes are fine.

And you talk too!

I was sad and tired. I am feeling better.

Come in, get some rest. We will talk in the morning.

It had been a long day. Leona was exhausted. She laid down and fell asleep immediately. She dreamed of the sea. She was traveling very fast, down, deep down. She felt like she was falling down so fast but she was not scared. She reached a very dark place and she could feel movements in the water, not really like waves but more like when someone moves close to you in the water. She could not see anyone but she felt a presence and she felt the urge to sing so she sang. She sang and felt at peace. She woke up sweating but her skin felt very dry. Dry and itchy. Her eyes were itchy too. She craved the sea. She knew it would make her feel better. She looked around and saw Lola's bed was empty. Her mother was not around either. Had she dreamed her? Had she ever been there at all? She stood up and stepped outside. She heard voices, singing and laughing. Lola and Freda were sitting under the mango tree in the backyard. They smiled at her when she approached them. Freda had washed a few mangoes and placed them in a bowl like she used to do for her back home.

Come eat, She said.

Leona sat between the two women and started eating.

You remember it wrong. Freda said. *I know what I wrote in that letter. My mother told me every detail, and I was there you know. I was only five but I remember. She walked back home at night, not in the morning. If she had walked back in the morning, everyone would have seen her and there would have been so many people coming to the house, but no, she came back at night and no-one was there. It was just the three of us and she could tell the whole story without interruption. She said she had broken her promise to the sea. She said it was the reason why she was taken to explain herself. She said Manman Dlo was disappointed about the broken promise and felt love for a man was not a strong enough reason not to keep her word. She said she apologised and promised to sing double what she should have been singing in a year. So she sang and sang. She sang non stop. She really felt sorry about not explaining herself to the drummer so he could understand and let her keep going to the sea. She felt guilty and decided she needed to redeem herself. She created new songs to ask for forgiveness and promise eternal gratitude. She closed her eyes and got lost into the music. There was nothing but* melody and rhythm. For a moment, nothing else existed. She was in a trance, immersed into the music. Then she started hearing her rhythm louder, but it was not being played by herself. She realised the drummer was playing. He was playing for her so she sang with a smile. She sang with all her heart and she felt better at first. Until she felt worst. The sound of his drum reminded her of what she was missing. She missed him and she missed me. She wanted to go back. She kept singing but she only sang when he played and she sounded good. They sounded good. These two were made to perform together and their music pleased Manman Dlo. She liked the way the griot smiled and danced when the drummer was playing but she didn't like the way she was sitting with her head in her hands, staring in the distance when he was not playing. She decided the griot had stayed there long enough and should go back up there. She asked her to go and told her to never forget her promise again.

She came back, at night, and told my father her whole story. He listened, nodded, frowned and shook his head. He didn't like it. He was happy to see her but he didn't like the story she *told him. He believed it, every word, but he didn't like it. How would he explain her sudden return to everyone? How would he explain that she was now going back to the sea again? How could he live with the fact that she had been taken as a consequence of his decision? How could he accept that she had kept all this information secret for so many years? He felt he had to make a decision immediately. He did not have any time to process all this information. As soon as someone, anyone, would see her, he would have to start answering questions and he was not ready to. He wanted her to never have been taken by the sea, never have received pearls, never have spoken a different language, never have come from the sea in the first place. How long did she say she had been in the sea? How old was she? He wanted her to be his age. He wanted her but he didn't want her. He wanted a life without any troubles. He knew it was not possible. Everyone has their fair share of troubles but who has troubles like the sea taking their woman away when she doesn't sing to her everyday? That's crazy troubles. He wanted a life without any crazy troubles. He sighted loudly and she understood. He told her he needed to think. He needed her to stay inside the house and talk to no-one while he went outside to think. She nodded and he left. He left like he had left before, for days and nights. She used to wait for him and worry all night when he did that. She used to worry until he came back but this time, she felt that maybe he would not come back at all. How long does it take to accept that someone is not coming back. One week? One month? One year? The longest he had ever left was around a week. It had been torture waiting for him that long and she didn't want to do it again. After a couple of days, she packed a bag, held my hand and we left. We went to the sea and took a small boat he had bought some time before. He had some fishermen friends who always wanted him to go fish with them. He always said he would go once he had a boat. One day, he bought a boat but he never used it. Fishing was not his thing. He was all about drumming, teaching drumming and maybe some odd jobs here and there. There was something about the sea he had never liked. He had bought the boat after deciding that he should be the only provider in the house. At the time, he was determined to make money any way possible, even fishing, but what happened was that the word spread that he was looking for work and people contacted him for what they knew he was good at. Anything music related, playing, teaching, repairing instruments and also gardening. So the boat just stayed there, unused. When my mother decided to go, it was there so we took it. I guess we stole it. My mother shook her hand in the water and the boat moved. We travelled all night I think. At some point, I fell asleep. When I woke up, the sun was rising and we had arrived here. My mother bought the house across from here. I think you know the rest of the story, right? Lola told you. And you went to the sea too, so you understand. You are like her, like my mother. I wish I could take the curse away from you but I can't. I tried. I tried really hard when I decided to move up to the mountain and keep you there with me. I tried but your body craved that sea water. It craved it so much you cried all the time and jumped into the river any chance you got. I knew what you needed but I didn't like it, never did. I never liked the sea, the way it kept my mother from having a normal life, the way it took her away when I was four, the way it lead my mother to beg me to not have any children and the way she ran back to it when I broke my promise. I never liked it.*

You know, when I saw you last night, soaked and happy, I felt like I was about to lose you too. I still feel it, I see it coming. You are feeling great, you are healed. There is no reason for you to come back home, right? Have you already decided to stay here? Do you want this kind of life? Sure the pearls, the money they bring, it's nice but believe me, the nasty looks and comments, they will ruin your life.

I have not received any pearls. I have been to the sea several times and received nothing. Maybe it's different for me.

Have you been singing?

No, not really. I mean, I have felt like I wanted to but I have not been singing.

Once you sing for real, if you don't receive any pearls then, I might believe it's different for you. I would be surprised though. You have been healed already. You have craved the sea your whole life. It doesn't seem different to me. I don't like it.

I don't like it either from what you and Lola are telling me. I don't want to be taken away and disappear under the sea, nor become a prisoner. I have not done anything wrong but I was punished when I could not see and my skin was itching and aching. Sure I feel better now but I am not sure it's worth it. I am scared. Maybe we should go home.

You are crying, Leona. I never liked to see you cry. No mother likes to see her child cry but me, I really always hated it. Because you never cried like any child. From day one, you always cried too much. No baby nor child I have ever seen cries so many tears. It's always been small rivers coming out of your eyes, even when you grew up and started crying silently just like you are doing now. These small rivers of tears look too much like my mother's huge rivers of tears, the ones that lead her back to the sea the last time I saw her. You are crying, Leona. You are crying and the sea is just there, a few steps away. I know what's coming next.

Leona furiously wiped the water off her face but her mother was right. A steady stream of tears kept coming. She could not stop it. Her skin was itching too. Any part of her skin that was untouched by her tears. It felt so uncomfortable and she knew what would immediately make her feel better. She knew but she did not want to prove her mother right. She wanted Freda to be wrong. She wanted it so bad but her whole body was screaming for the sea. She shook her arms, wiped her face with her hands once, twice, many times.

Don't fight it. Freda said. *I see you can't focus. Go get some relief, we'll talk later.*

Leona nodded and tried her best to look relaxed and not too eager. She fought against her instinct to run out the house instead of walking. She closed the door slowly and started walking. After a few steps, she looked back and saw no-one was watching so she started running. She ran and ran and jumped into the sea. Oh the relief! The satisfaction! The happiness! The pure joy! How good the water felt on her skin, in her eyes, her ears, her mouth. She could open her mouth wide, have water invading her nostrils and feel no discomfort. She was coming to terms with that reality. It was natural, her natural state to be that comfortable in the sea. She stayed still and rested for a while. She felt like her body was being rocked back and forth. She closed her eyes and fell asleep. She dreamed again, the same dream, except this time she saw something or someone, a transparent silhouette circling around her. She could feel the water moving around the silhouette. She had to concentrate, squinting her eyes to see better but she couldn't understand what or who it was. She heard some kind of sound, like a melody or a rhythm. Sound is different under the water, there was some kind of echo. She felt very confused. She closed her eyes to concentrate on the sound until she could hear a distinct melody accompanied by a rhythm. She felt like she had heard it before. She knew the words and the harmony came out of her effortlessly. She clapped along with the rhythm and danced. She sang the song again and again. She danced and danced like she had never danced before. She couldn't help herself; it was as though she was hypnotised. The more she sang, the better she felt. She sang and sang until she felt a presence very close to her. She opened her eyes and saw the silhouette more clearly, it looked like the body of a woman. She stopped clapping, dancing and singing. The silhouette was trying to touch her. Her hand was getting so close. Leona suddenly became scared. She tried to swim away but she felt heavy, she could not move. She shook her head left and right, trying to scream but no sound was coming out. A hand grabbed her and took her out of the water. The morning sun blinded her, she was lying on something hard. Two hands were on her shoulders. She started fighting her attacker.

Calm down. I mean no harm, ok?

She woke up for good and realised she was in a small boat, lying next to smelly dead fishes. She looked at the man who just talked.

Did you kill all these fishes?

Well that's my job. I am a fisherman.

She sat up and looked around. They were pretty far away from the beach. She started estimating how long it would take her to go back if she jumped right now. He looked amused.

Are you thinking about jumping back in there to escape me? I did not attack you, you know. I actually saved you. You looked like you were drowning so I got you out of there. I think Thank You is the appropriate response here.

I was not drowning. I was doing just fine.

It's a bit far to be swimming alone. There are strong currents here, you know. It's dangerous. You should be more careful.

I am an excellent swimmer. I was doing just fine.

You didn't look like it, sorry. You look tired too. I'm going back now. Please don't try drowning again. Let me take you to the beach, ok?

She was exhausted. It had been a very vivid dream and she had no clue how long it had lasted. All she knew was she was tired and hungry.

Ok.

You are not from here, right? I have never seen you before.

Hmm.

Do you often swim that early in the morning and alone?

Hmm.

I see, you're not very talkative. Not very grateful either.

Thank you for helping me. I guess I am a bit tired.

Here you go! That was not so hard, right?

Hmm.

He laughed.

I got it. No more talking for today. Let's go, Miss Tired Mermaid.

When they reached the beach, she hurried out of the boat, thanked him, washed her face in sea water and marched back to Lola's house. It was a brisk walk. She wanted to run, put as much distance as possible between him and her but she wanted him to think she was unbothered. She wasn't.

She was quite upset. She was angry with herself for not having found the words to shut him up when he questioned her swimming abilities, when he looked so amused and when he laughed. He found her in a tricky situation and he found it entertaining. No doubt he was going to talk to his friends about the strange girl he found in the sea. A girl who could barely swim but thought she could go far from the beach, early in the morning when there was no one around to rescue her. Luckily, he was coming back from his fishing trip to save the silly girl. They were all going to have a good laugh. She felt angry. He didn't know her. How dare he judge her!

She remembered all these years growing up alone with her mother. It had always been just the two of them and that was how she was comfortable. She hated when they were separated. She hated leaving in the morning to go to school. All these kids pointing and laughing, calling her a cry baby and turning their backs on her anytime she found the courage to try and approach them. It looked like fun, having friends, playing. Most of the time, she thought they were mean kids and she was happy to avoid them, but sometimes, she looked at them with envy and daydreamed about running around with them. Jumping up and down and screaming with joy. She liked the songs too. She really liked the songs. Some of the girls were always singing, clapping their hands and stomping their feet. She used to sit behind a tree, far enough for them not to notice her but close enough to hear the songs. She would memorise the lyrics and the melodies, maybe hum a little if she felt she was far enough for them not to hear her. Then she would go home and sing in the garden. She would sing with her eyes closed and her troubles would go away. Her skin wouldn't itch, her eyes would get wet but no tear would fall. Singing was the only thing that made her feel peaceful. Better than crying in secret, better than swimming in the river. Remembering this made her smile. It was not all bad up there. Maybe she didn't need the sea, maybe she could go back home and just sing more. Singing in the sea was amazing of course but it ended up being so scary. She was not sure she wanted to go again. Her skin still felt good from the sea water and she could smell the waves on her skin. It felt good. Maybe she could stay here and only have very small baths very close to the beach. Maybe she could go at night to avoid any noisy fishermen. She was very confused and unsure about what the best next step should be but she was sure of one thing. She would always have singing to ground herself and make life bearable wherever she decided to go.

When she reached Lola's house, she was feeling better. She didn't go in but walked around and sat under a tree in Lola's garden. She closed her eyes and sang. She sang the song from the sea and the same feeling of peace came over her. She felt at ease. Her mother joined her and sang a low harmony. She opened her eyes and stared at her in surprise.

How do you know this song?

My mother used to sing it all the time. She sang it on her way to the sea every single day for many years. I had to stay on the beach and watch her disappear in the waves while she was singing this song. I watched her do that for years and years but every single time, I was terrified. I always felt like maybe this time she would not come back. She raised me near to the sea so I knew how to swim. I played in the sea with my friend. We dared each other to stay under water to see who could last the longest and we came back, gasping for air and laughing. At some point, I stopped this game. It was not fun to me anymore. I could see that nobody could last a long time under water, but my mother, she used to walk to the sea until her head went under. She used to stay there for at least an hour every single day. I thought maybe it was a gift, maybe it was a curse. I thought one day, she'll think she can do it as usual but the gift will be taken away and she will be like us, dying to come back up for air. What if this happened when she was too far away down there? What would happen then? Would she stay stuck down in the sea? What would happen to me? Who would take care of me? I was a child and I had no father. She never told me what happen with him. I didn't even know if he was alive. I had no family, only her and she was risking her life every single day. At first, she never wanted to answer my questions when I asked about why she was doing that, where she was going. I was scared, I needed to understand. One day, I asked her how she knew she was not going to die under the water. I told her I didn't want to be an orphan. She said I wouldn't be and she would always be there to take care of me. I said I didn't believe her because nobody can breathe under water. She smiled and said there is a lot many people don't know. I asked more questions and she kept dancing around them, never giving me any clear response. I became resentful. I stopped playing with kids, I pushed them away, by ignoring them or by being mean to them sometimes. I wanted to be alone. The only one who still wanted to be my friend was Lola. She was patient. She understood something was wrong and she gave me time and space to be by myself and figure things out. My mother used to go to the sea early in the morning, when it was still the night and everyone was asleep. I was supposed to stay in bed but I always followed her. When she stayed in the water too long, I used to cry. Silently at first and then more and more loudly. One morning, I was screaming at the top of my lungs:

Mama! Mama come back! Mama!

Some neighbours heard me and came over. They asked where my mother was and I understood I had made a big mistake. They took their boats and started looking for her in the water. I cried and cried so much. I knew we would be in trouble once she'd come back. Still a part of me thought maybe this was the day she would not come back but she did. Everybody had been looking for her for maybe 15-20 minutes and there she was, coming out of the water, confused, asking everyone what they were doing. She said she had just gone for a quick bath and everyone started looking at her in a strange way. Their mouths said they understood but their eyes said otherwise. They had no explanation for what was going on and they didn't like it. They didn't like it at all. They thought it was suspicious, maybe dangerous and they decided to stay away to protect themselves. They decided to protect their families by telling everyone to stay away from us, even the children, even Lola. Her parents told her not to play with me anymore. We were alone and it was all my fault. I cried at night and my mother would say it was not my fault. She said it was normal for me to be scared. She said I should not be scared and she would tell me why. And she did.

She explained everything to me. Where she came from, how she was saved by Manman Dlo, how she promised to sing and where her money came from. She said she would break her promise for me. She said, once people see that the baths have stopped, they would treat me right as they did before. Early in the morning, she opened a window and showed me who was keeping an eye on the beach to see if she was going for a swim. We kept waking up early every morning, out of habit, but we didn't leave the house until the sun was fully up. We would then go have breakfast in the garden, smile and greet loudly anyone who would be passing by. At first, they would ignore us and cross the street but after my mother started selling her fruits in the market, people would start greeting us back. Slowly everything went back to normal. We had less money but less animosity towards us too. We were part of the village, like everybody else. We never talked about the sea again. Her vision started diminishing, her skin became *very dry and she became depressed. She didn't like singing*

and talking so much anymore. She was just sad and tired. It

was all my fault. She was always healthy and happy before

and it had all stopped because of me. She became more and

more silent. She stopped talking to buyers at the markets, to

neighbours and finally she stopped talking to me. The only

time she broke her silence was when I became a woman. She

explained to me that my body could now make a child but I

should never do it. She said I should stay away from men, that

if I ever had a child, the child would be like her and owe the

sea daily visits and songs. She said the child would suffer like

she did if she did not keep her promise. She explained when

she was taken by a wave to see Manman Dlo the first time she

stopped singing, she had to explain herself. The promise was

amended and she was told her skin and eyes would crave the

sea if she avoided her responsibilities again. She said no child

deserved to suffer like she did, from judgement from others or

from a body who does not want to be out of the sea for too

long. She made me promise to never have children. I was

upset with her at that point, because I could never be out with my friends, living the kind of life they lived was out of reach. I was looking at them from my window and feeling like my life was on pause. I always had to be home, trying to help her with everything because I felt guilty for causing her troubles. I felt guilty but still I was angry with her, so when she asked me to promise I would never have children, I said yes so she would leave me alone. I didn't want to hear any more of her story. I wanted to know nothing more about all that. I wanted to be like everyone else. I wanted to be someone else, in a family with both a mother and a father. A family with no song to sing to the sea. I knew for a very long time that I wanted a family and I wanted it to be different, much different from what I had known so far. She was telling me I couldn't have that and I was not ready to hear it, so I said yes to stop the conversation. I swore with my fingers crossed behind my back. I swore so she would leave me alone and never talk about this again. And she never talked to me again. Until the last day I saw her, she never talked to me again.

Freda turned her gaze in the direction of the sea and sighed.

I am going to go now. I don't like being around the sea for too long. I don't like the sight of it, the smell, the sound. I just don't like it. I feel better up there - she waved in the direction of the mountain - *it's quiet. It's peaceful, but it's not for everyone. You don't have to like it too. It's ok if you don't want to come home. Here is some money and the keys of my mother's house. I know it's not looking good right now but this is enough money to fix it up and I know I taught you what you need to know to grow whatever fruit or vegetable you want. Just go to the market and see what's missing, or what's not sweet enough and grow that. You will be fine.*

She got up and went back inside the house. Leona followed her and saw her take her bag, which was already near the door. Freda got out with Lola by her side. They walked slowly to the large road that went up to the mountain, Leona following them, wondering if she should say something, run to Lola's house to grab her bag and go back home too. She thought about it but Freda and Lola were already saying goodbye. Then Leona looked at the sea and wondered if she could maybe get some sea water in a bottle or two and go home with that. Maybe she could come back here once a week or so and fill her bottles. Maybe she could do that. She was thinking about it but Freda was ready to go now. Maybe swimming in the river and singing could be good enough. Freda and Lola were done with their long goodbyes. Maybe she could just cry more in silence like she used to, it had always felt good. Not as good as the sea but good. Her mother was waving goodbye and smiling sadly. Leona ran to her and hugged her. Freda said:

Stop crying. You don't need to cry anymore. Just get into that water whenever you feel you need it. No more crying for salty water now. Just be careful when you get in there. I am happy I did not keep my promise. I am happy I had you. I hope my mother sees you. She will understand it was worth it.

She started walking but stopped and looked at Leona a last time. A sad smile and a weak wave, that's the last memory Leona had from her mother. She'd always regret not going back home with her on that day, even at first, when everything was perfect, when life was sweet and easy. Even then, there was always something deep inside telling her that she should have gone back to the mountain.

11

Freda was right, there was more than enough money to have the house fixed up. Lola knew everyone and introduced Leona to anyone who could help. Leona cleaned up the garden behind the house after going to the market and finding out that nobody was growing any flowers. She started growing some. Beautiful, colourful and fragrant flowers, medicinal herbs too. Lola knew a lot about that and taught her. She walked to the market and started selling them. She heard people whispering « *the daughter of the florist* » and smiled when they complimented her herbs and flowers. She easily fell into a routine. Sea bath early in the morning and also late at night. Her eyes and her skin felt and looked amazing. She was singing too, at first while gardening mainly. She was trying her best not to sing while bathing into the sea but the impulse was strong. Eventually, she was humming, just a little bit to begin with and only with her head out of the water. Then, humming under water. Swimming away whenever she'd hear any rhythm. Swimming away whenever she'd see any silhouette. Swimming away too when she spotted the fisherman's boat. He'd wave at her from afar and she'd swim away. She would lay awake at night, thinking about the drummer who left to think and maybe never came back, maybe came back to an empty house. She would think about the florist, who thought he'd start a big family. He thought he could talk Sila into accepting her daughter who could have a normal life. Alone or dead. Men had been unlucky with the women of her family. This silly fisherman surely shouldn't experience the same fate. She would swim away anytime she saw him but she would also lay awake at night thinking of him. She'd feel so annoyed with herself. So annoyed she'd sometimes need to get up and go for a swim to get some peace of mind.

It was on one of those nights when she forgot about her self-inflicted rules. She closed her eyes and let the waves rock her softly. She fell asleep and slipped into bliss. She opened her mouth to the salt of the sea and sang. She heard a rhythm and did not swim away. She saw the water moving and did not swim away. She felt a touch on her arm and did not try to escape. She kept on singing and clapping and dancing. She twirled and twirled down to the bottom of the sea and she sat down there, peaceful.

She smiled. Someone was there. She could not see clearly but she was not afraid.

Finally - a voice said. *I have been waiting for you for a long time. I see you in the water everyday but you have been swimming away from me every day. I was not going to chase you, little girl. I knew one day you would come to accept who you are but I never thought it would take you so long.*

I can't see you. I hear you, I feel you are there but I can't see you.

A hand grabbed her and pulled her up until she reached the surface. The moon was high and round in the sky, giving enough light so she could see the woman in front of her. A face looked familiar. She looked like her mother but she actually looked more like Leona herself. She understood what she had suspected down there was correct. This is Sila, the griot, her grand mother. Sila smiled and said.

So you are done running away from me?

I was not running away. I was just ready to go home.

You were not scared?

No I wasn't.

You looked like it.

Well I wasn't.

That was the conversation with the fisherman all over again. Leona wondered why she always had to do that, deny the obvious. Anytime she found herself in a tricky situation and was scared or confused, she'd pretend she had everything under control. She could not ask for help nor admit she was in trouble. Always trying to act strong. Was it from all the name calling with all her crying? She was tired of people thinking she was weak. Thinking about it annoyed her and she was not good at hiding her emotions.

No need to get upset. Let's say I believe you. You were not scared. At least, you are not now. I brought you something.

She took Leona's hand and placed a couple of pearls in it.

This is to thank you for the singing.

I don't want it. I am not going to come and sing here everyday.

You don't have to.

I don't have to? I thought that was the promise. My mother told me...

She told you what she knew but things change. She told you that I gave up walking the earth? Why do you think I did that?

Because she had broken her promise and you did not want to see me be born.

Is that what your mother told you?

No but this is what she thinks. This is what it looks like to me.

Well you are wrong, both of you. I came back to the sea to try and change the promise. I had promised I would sing everyday and my grand baby would sing everyday too. I had promised this in exchange of being able to walk the earth again. Now that I am back to the sea, it has to be different. Now you don't have to sing everyday. You are bound to the water but, if you want, you can just swim a bit and go back to your life. And, if you want, you can sing too. You can receive pearls here and there if your song pleases Manman. You can choose to stay with me too. You choose what you want to do.

That's the reason why I decided to come back to the sea,

because I knew this way I would be able to give you options.

You don't have to live like I did.

Leona opened her hand and looked at the pearls.

They are beautiful. Thank you.

You deserve them. You sing beautifully. Listen, I need you to

go wherever your mother decided to go. I need you to talk to

her. Let her know why I left. I need her to know. Will you do

this for me?

Of course, yes, I will go in the morning.

Good. I'd better go now. I see your friend is coming this way.

She dived back in the sea and Leona turned around. The
fisherman was just a bit further away, waving from afar so she
swam away and went home to pack a bag. She knocked on
Lola's door and let her know she was going home for the day.

On her way up, her skin started to feel itchy and she panicked. She ran home and grabbed two empty bottles, ran to the sea, wet her face and arms, then she filled up her bottles.

The more she walked, the more she could see the vegetation become denser. She could hear the sound of the sea slowly disappear. Walking up the road to go home, she remembered every tree, every bush but they all seemed to be bigger. Only a few months had passed but it felt like a lifetime. As she approached the house, she could hear some voices, singing and clapping. She recognised the song immediately but did not want to believe what it meant. She understood but did not want to. She slowed her pace, stopped to rest when she was not tired. The song grew louder and louder. She recognised the voices of this and that neighbour. As she reached the house, she recognised their faces too. Some opened their arms to welcome and comfort her but she pushed them away. She pushed away anyone in her path and entered her mother's bedroom to find her lying in bed in her best dress. Cold and lifeless.

What happened? What happened? What happened?

That was all she could say. She didn't understand. Last time she saw her, she was healthy. It was not such a long time ago. She was fine. She had lived all these years thinking Sila was likely dead. She thought Sila had been so angry at her she had preferred going to the sea to die or be a prisoner. Today Leona had come back to give her good news. Sila was well and alive. She was not angry. She had left to change the promise and make Leona's life easier. This was good news. She had come to give her mother good news but she was too late. Her strong, healthy mother was lying there, lifeless. What happened? That's all she could say.

When she came back from visiting you, she said she was tired and needed to rest her body. She said the sea made her sick. She has been in bed since. We have visited her and brought the doctor but he couldn't find anything wrong with her. We thought about going to get you but she wouldn't say where you were. Yesterday, I found her.

Leona did not know who had spoken. She did not understand what they said except the sea made her sick. Freda had always hated the sea. The sea between her and her father. The sea who took her mother and the man she loved. The sea she believed had been about to take her daughter too. She went home, by herself, and laid there, thinking of how much the sea had taken from her. She laid there, tired. She was resting now.

For once, Leona could cry all she wanted and nobody had any comment to make, so she cried and cried. She cried through the wake and the funeral. She cried long after that too. She cried until her eyes started feeling dry. She used the bottles of sea water to wet her eyes and ease her skin. When the bottles were empty, she closed the house and went down, back to the sea. She left her bag on the beach and walked straight into the waves. She did not sing nor clap nor dance. She just laid there, letting the sea heal her skin and eyes. She had been suffering for a while when she decided to return. She had been so uncomfortable during the long walk back. All she wanted was some relief. The sea held her and rocked her until she fell asleep. She opened her eyes and felt Sila beside her. She felt her hand on her shoulder and cried. Sila held her and said:

I know. I felt it when it happened. I am sorry.

She said the sea made her sick. This is the last thing she said. It is my fault. It is because I chose to stay here. I chose the sea over her, like she thought you chose the sea over her.

You know I did not choose the sea over her.

I know but she didn't. You never came back to explain anything to her. She died thinking everyone abandoned her.

I did not choose the sea over her. I chose to give her and you both a better life.

Without any explanation.

There was silence for a while. Leona wondered if Sila was crying, if she could even cry. She tried as before to focus, squinting her eyes to see her better but she still couldn't. Sila was still and Leona could not even tell where she was. Was she even still there? She felt her hand on her shoulder again. This time she pushed it away. She didn't want comfort. She wanted to scream and kick. She closed her eyes and tried to calm down.

I want to be alone.

She didn't want to be alone really. She wanted to be away from Sila. She wanted her gone. Sila moved away. Leona could see a wave rushing away. At the same time, she heard:

Come here and call me, anytime.

Leona moved up, high enough to see that the sky was dark now but there was just a little bit of light in the east. It was going to be sunrise soon. She had always loved watching the sunrise. The changing colours of the sky always appeased her. It gave her hope that things could get better in a world where such beauty was available to all. She reached the surface and watched the first ray of sun make the water glisten.

Good morning, miss tired mermaid. How are you feeling today? Do you need a ride?

It was him. She recognised his voice. The sun had started warming her heart and she was no longer angry. She had lied to Sila. She didn't want to be alone. She wanted company and she was tired of swimming away from him.

Good morning. I am not tired and I don't need a ride, thank you.

He said he was watching the sunrise too and invited her to sit and watch with him.

I saw you many times, early in the morning. I tried to say hello but you always swam away. I am only trying to get to know you, I have to say, it hurt my feelings when you don't return my greeting.

Well, that's one thing to know about me. I am a bit rude sometimes.

He laughed.

I must be crazy because I still want your company.

They sat in silence until the sun was fully out. Then he told her stories about sailing to different parts of the sea, about storms and hurricanes. He told her he saw a mermaid once and she looked like her. She wondered if he was lying and decided she didn't care. He was a good storyteller, entertaining, distracting her from what had just happened in the mountain and from what had happened down in the sea. She didn't want to think about any of it. She wanted to forget and he was helping her do just that. They went back to the beach and agreed to meet back there after she'd quickly gone home and he had sold his fish to his usual market seller.

Leona went to greet Lola and tell her the news about her mother. Lola lit a candle and they sat in silence. Leona felt that Lola looked sad but not surprised.

Are you not surprised? She was fine last time we saw her. Are you not angry she didn't want to say where I was? We could have gone to see her before it was too late. We could have gone together!

I am surprised she left so soon but I am not surprised of the way she chose to go. Freda has always done things her own way. Once she decided what she wanted to do, no one could ever make her change her mind, and she was always good at keeping secrets too. I am not very surprised, no, but I am sad of course. She was my friend.

She was my mom.

You have a family here now, you know. Everyone loves you. You can always come to me for anything and I am sure many others will be happy to help with anything you need. Anytime you want to talk or anything else.

I know, but I am not sure I will stay. It's because of what she said. She said the sea made her sick. She died hating the sea. Staying here kind of feels like a betrayal.

You are not your mother. She hated the sea but you love it. You need it. Are you ready to lose your sight again, just because you think your mother didn't want you in the sea? She told you you could stay. She saw how much better you felt here. I think she would want you to stay where you are healthy. You could be happy here.

I don't know.

Give it a try at least. Look how long it took you to come and see me. Can you tell me that you were not in the sea all night? I know how good it makes you feel and your mother knew it too. I would hate to know you are suffering up there, away from the sea. Give it some thought and let's talk about it in a few weeks at least, ok?

Leona shook her head yes and smiled as she remembered the feeling of the sea water on her skin, the sunrise on the sea and her talk with the fisherman. She remembered their agreement and said goodbye to Lola. She walked back to the sea, ready for more stories, ready to forget about making any decision.

12

Ida hadn't slept so well in years, since Maya was born, since the traveler was gone, since all of her troubles had started. She had worried so much ever since. She was having dreams of huge waves taking the traveler away, taking Maya away, huge waves going up like a wall and preventing her from going after her loved ones. She was having so many of these dreams that she had come to dread the night. She was tired, exhausted but she didn't want to sleep. She didn't want those dreams. She had tried many things like prayer and meditation, changing her diet, exercising before bed. Any new attempt always seemed to work for one night or two but the dreams always came back. It should have made her hate the sea but no, she was just as fascinated as she had always been.

Growing up in the mountain with Leona, she had heard her schoolmates talking about their visits to family members near the sea and she had always wanted to go. There had been a couple of school trips to the sea but Leona had not allowed her to go. She had said the sea was not safe. She had said:

Maybe one day, when you grow up. Maybe one day.

But the day never came and Ida had many river baths dreaming about the big blue sea. She had imagined the salty taste in her mouth and the sun coming down, as if it was going to sleep under the sea. After all these years, even with the bad dreams, when Ida woke up every morning, she was happy she could listen to the sound of the waves. She was secretly happy Maya needed the sea so much, this way she had an extra reason to go everyday, several times a day if needed. She could sit there for ages and look at it, mesmerised. Any resentment at all for the dreams and how tired she felt always faded when she admired the dance of the waves.

When she had reached her mother's house, she was as tired as always but, as usual, she wasn't expecting to get any good sleep. But time time, as soon as her head touched the pillow, her eyes closed and she had a good long restful night. She woke up refreshed and surprised. It took her a moment to remember where she was and why she was there. She looked around and couldn't find Maya so she stood up and started searching the house. Maya was outside with Leona, singing under a mango tree. She was singing a song Leona used to sing when Ida was a child. Ida used to think her mother had the most beautiful voice. She had bragged about it at school once and had been called a liar because nobody had ever heard Leona sing. When she went home crying about it, Leona told her that she didn't like to sing around people, that her singing was for Ida only, a secret thing just between the two of them. Ida couldn't understand why but she liked having a secret so she never talked about it ever again.

That morning, she walked quietly to meet them and listened to Maya sing along. She was just a child but she sounded good already. The lyrics and the melody came back to Ida and she joined in too. They sat together and sang for a while.

It was a song to the sea. Ida always wondered why her mother sang a song to the sea when she never went to the beach and had never allowed her to go. It didn't make sense but it was a beautiful song. She had listened to this song and sung along all these years and never asked the question. She had always felt she shouldn't ask. She felt it would upset her mother. She didn't know why; it was just a feeling she had. Maybe she had been wrong all these years. It was just a question. She could say no if she didn't want to explain. She could lie and say she forgot where it came from. Or she could tell the truth. Before she could think about it, she heard the words coming out of her mouth:

Why do you always sing this song? I thought you hated the sea?

I don't hate the sea, but my mother did. She really did. Bad things happened to her. Bad things always linked to the sea, so she decided to come here to stay away from it.

But the song, was she singing the song even if she hated the sea? Did she teach you the song?

No, my grand-mother taught me the song.

You never told me about your grand-mother. What was her name?

Her name was Sila. She was a great singer, an amazing one and she used to sing to the sea.

What happened to her?

A bad thing in the sea.

Ida was anxious to know more. Leona didn't want to elaborate, being used to keeping secrets but Ida wanted answers, clear ones, now.

Mama, a bad thing linked to the sea has happened to me too and a good thing too. I want to tell you everything but will you talk to me too?

Of course, I always knew this day would come. Maya told me about the sea, her eyes and the pearls. Nothing surprising to me. She didn't tell me about her father. She doesn't seem to remember him.

You remember him right? He was a traveller. Always on a boat, buying and selling in different islands. He was supposed to come home on the day Maya was born but there was a storm and he didn't make it. Pieces of his boat were found but not him. He never came back.

I am sorry, Leona. I tried to warn you. There is nothing but heartbreak out there in the sea. Now you said a good thing happened. Are you talking about the pearls?

Yes, Maya told you.

She told me and I was not surprised. I received many pearls myself when I was still going to the sea. At first, I thought it was a good thing too. I enjoyed all the benefits of it but then I decided to come back here.

Why? Why stay here and work so hard when you could go to the sea and be taken care of?

Why did you run away from your house and come here?

People were wondering and I didn't want to explain. Also, I had dreams about you.

What kind of dreams?

Just seeing you. It made me realise how much I missed you and how sorry I was for leaving like I did. Also, I thought you might want to see Maya.

You thought right. It brings me a lot of joy to see her, and you too, but you came for answers too, right?

Yes, I want to know about my father and his family. I wanted to know if they had any eye problems. I thought it could explain what is happening with Maya but now I see it's our side of the family.

Yes, it's all us. I am like Maya. My mother was like you. My grand-mother was like Maya and me. It's a blessing and a curse.

Do you mean you were not always blind?

Leona turned to face where the sound of Maya playing was coming from.

Baby, bring me the bottle you told me about.

Maya ran to the house and came back with one of the bottles of sea water. Leona used it to wash her face. She then poured a little bit of water directly in her eyes. She kept them close for a while then rubbed and opened them. The white film over her cornea disappeared. Leona waved her hands in front of her frantically.

Mama, can you see me? Do you see me?

I see you like Maya can see you. I was never really blind. It was a choice I made to honour my mother's memory. She hated the sea. She hated knowing I was out there so I decided to come back here and bear the consequences.

Leona couldn't believe her eyes but mainly, she couldn't believe her ears. She didn't understand Leona's decisions and felt maybe she would judge her for making different ones.

Do you mean that you think this is what I should do and Maya too? To honour your mother?

I don't want to tell you what to do. My mother gave me choices. She made sure I knew the whole story and then allowed me to make my own decisions. I want to do the same. The difference is that, when you make your decision, I don't want you to think of me too much. I want you to think about what is best for you and your child.

So what is the story? The whole story.

Leona started talking. She talked about Sila's songs. The ones she sang on the boat, under the water and on the beach when she met the drummer. She talked about what happened when she stopped singing to the water, when she came back and moved to this island. She talked about Freda, growing up taking care of a blind and barely speaking mother. She talked about the florist, how he and Sila disappeared in the sea. She talked about Freda running away to the mountain. She talked about herself, growing up with skin and eye issues until she became blind and depressed. She talked about her time with

Lola, her time under the water and her decision to stay near the sea, how this decision killed Freda. She cried a little and talked some more. She talked about the fisherman and smiled.

Then why didn't you stay with him? What made you come here?

I used to talk to Sila all the time. She knew me better than I knew myself. When I became pregnant, she knew it immediately. She was the one who told me. She reminded me of how things were going to be. You would have a normal life but your child would be like me. I thought of how lucky I was to have met your father who didn't care about how unusual I was. He found it funny that I seemed to like the sea even more than he did. I never told him everything so he really thought that I simply really loved the sea, or maybe he half guessed what was happening and never told me. I almost never used the pearls because I knew how it had turned out for Sila. Instead, I worked hard in my garden and sold my flowers.

People came from far to buy my flowers and my herbs so I was doing well. I didn't need any pearls. There has been a couple of times, after big storms, when people wouldn't buy them. These were the only times I would sell the pearls. I'd pretend people in the city would buy my herbs and go there. Then, I'd throw the herbs away and go to a jewellery shop to sell my pearls instead. I thought it could go on like this. I really thought we could be happy forever. I thought we could have this baby, who would live a life like any other baby. We could do that and worry about the grand-baby when the day comes. If it ever came. Some people do not want children. Some want them but cannot have them. I thought maybe I could forget about the potential grand-baby and keep on living my happy life.

But one day, as I was on my way to the city after some bad times on the market, someone saw me throw the herbs away and told him. When I came back home with the money, he asked me where it came from. He called me a liar and told me to admit I was selling my body to big city men. I couldn't let him believe that so I told him the truth. He didn't believe me at first but I forced him to follow me to the sea. When I came back with pearls, he had to believe me. He went to the neighbour who had seen me and told him a story about me having a rich grand-mother in the city. He said I had lied because I knew he wouldn't accept to be treated like a charity by my rich family members. The neighbour bought it and they never spoke on this again. He never looked at me the same way again. He was angry. He felt stupid because we had spent years together and I had let him think that I was normal, as he said. He started resenting me every time I went out to the sea. He didn't like to hear me sing anymore. I tried being more understanding, cooking his favourite foods, asking him to tell me his favourite stories, not saying anything when he got home late, cheering more when he had a good day at sea but nothing worked. Once the trust was broken, there was nothing I could do to restore it. So when Sila told me I was pregnant, instead of thinking I could worry about the potential grand-baby later, I started worrying about what my child's life was going to be. Would he spend his time looking at her with disdain too? Would he constantly wonder if she was abnormal

too? Would he never trust her, never love her? Would he be

able to love the child of an abnormal lying woman?

I had dreams of my mother telling me how she didn't like to

be close to the sea for too long. This is one of the last things

she told me the last time I saw her alive. I remembered how

peaceful it is here. Sila could see what was on my mind and

tried to remind me of why I had wanted so badly to run away

from this place, but nothing she could say was convincing

enough for me to want to stay. The pain of losing my sight and

being uncomfortable in my skin was nothing compared to the

heartbreak caused by the way your father was looking at me.

It was too much. I couldn't bare it. I still had a little bit of hope.

I was still waking up in the morning, hoping it would be a

different day. I daydreamed about him saying that he forgave

me and accepted me for who I was. I dreamed of things going

back to the way they were before but days and weeks passed

and it did not happen. I woke up one morning and told him I

loved him. He looked at me with sadness in his eyes and said he wasn't sure he could ever love me again. He said he felt he

didn't know me anymore. All he knew about me was that I was

a liar. Then he said he had to work, got his fishing gear and

made me swear to never get any pearls again. He asked me to

stay in the house. He didn't want any neighbour to ask me

any questions.

I opened the window and watched him leave. He always left

before sunrise. I could barely see him under the moonlight;

but I could hear. I could hear the sea so well that I heard the

boat when it started moving on it. I heard it sail away. When

he was far enough, I went to see Sila and cried on her

shoulder. She was angry, she said a storm was coming and I'd

be better off without him. She had never liked him. She had

always tried to convince me to leave him. She had worked so

hard to hold her « I told you so » when everything had gone

bad but now, she couldn't hold it anymore. She said she knew

that day was coming, the day he would break my heart. Then

she started talking about my pregnancy, how it was bad for

the baby for me to be sad while pregnant, that everybody

knows that, he knows that but he is causing me heartbreak anyway. I had to stop her and confess he didn't know. I had not told him yet. I was about to tell him but then everything went wrong and I didn't want him to think I was using the baby to change the subject and force him to forgive me. I wanted him to forgive me because he loved me, for no other reason. I wanted him to at least try to understand me, but he didn't; He didn't understand me and he didn't forgive me. He said he might never love me again. I cried and cried again. The more upset I got, the angrier the sea appeared to be. I was in a bubble with Sila but all around us, I could see the waves rising and falling down furiously. My heart was pounding, I was sad and angry. I asked Sila to find the fisherman and save him but she didn't move. All she was saying was that I needed to calm down. She sang softly to me. She sang a sweet quiet song. I had to focus to hear the melody over the sound of the angry sea. The more I focused on the song, the calmer I and the sea became.

You don't have to worry about him. Sila said - the storm has passed. You need to stay here with me for a while if you want to learn how to master your emotions. It's dangerous for other people if you get upset in or near the sea and cannot calm yourself down.

I was not ready to listen to anything more she had to say. I had not asked for all of this. I had personally made no promise to anyone. Sure, it felt great to be in the sea and sing. I was very grateful for the pearls anytime I needed them but this promise, this secret, it was costing me my relationship and now, on the top of that, I was finding out I could be a danger for the man I loved and for everyone else. My emotions could create dangerous storms; and the only way I could control this was to stay under the sea for a while when I had promised I wouldn't go anymore! No, that was too much, just too much. The sun was about to rise and I knew this meant he was going to come home soon, so I left, got home and changed. I did my best to calm myself down and think about a solution. I couldn't come up with anything. The only thing I could do to maybe have him forgive me would be to avoid the sea and be back in an itchy skin, lose my sight. Would he love me back or feel this was some additional abnormal condition? Or I could sneak out when he was at sea like I had just done. But then I would have to endure conversations with Sila trying to convince me to leave him and stay with her under the water. I was starting to wonder if she was telling me the truth. Maybe she was the one creating storms to make me think I needed time with her to learn how to control water. She had broken her promise to Manman Dlo before. What was a lie to me in comparison? I wasn't sure I could trust her to tell me the truth. I wasn't sure I could trust that time would help him forgive me one day. I would have loved my mother to be there to advise me. She had always been brutally honest. Some people didn't like it but at least you always knew where she stood and her advice always made sense. She had decided to leave and go start a new life in the mountain. It was a good life, for the most part. I had had some challenges. Kids had made fun of me, found me strange but adults had been nice to me. They had been even nicer when I had lost my sight, even kids had been *nicer. If I go back - I thought - they could be nice again. They had never harassed my mother with questions about my father. Maybe they'll do the same for me. I could have my perfect baby there and live a good life. I could grow fruits and herbs. I could have a good life. That's what was on my mind when your father came back from work. He looked at me, hesitated, opened his mouth to speak but said nothing, closed it and turned around. I said:*

Do you want me to leave?

He stopped and without looking at me, he said:

You are not a prisoner. I can't stop you if you want to leave.

That's not what I asked. I said do you want me to leave?

Today, yes. But I don't know if that's what I will want tomorrow.

He left and I knew what I was going to do. I packed my bags, said good bye to Lola and came here. I was welcomed back like a long lost family member. Everybody helped me fix up the house. I was given the same place in the market where I used to go with my mother. There were a few questions about my growing belly but I used my mother's response:

I am here to start a new life, not talk about the past.

People laughed and said:

I swear I can hear Freda in your voice.

When my sight deteriorated, nobody was surprised. I was good old Leona, child of Freda. I was like they had known me before and I was actually accepted as I was, still am. My skin doesn't even bother me that much anymore and my sight, well, I know this house, the garden and the market like the back of my hand and there is nowhere else I want to go so I don't care about my sight really. I am happy I can see your faces today but if I don't see them anymore, I have them in my mind so that's alright.

So you think I should let Maya loose her sight too?

I am not telling you what to do. I am telling you what I decided to do for myself. What you want to do for you and your child is not my decision.

Do you still think Sila cannot be trusted?

I don't know. I wonder everyday. Sometimes I feel like maybe I have been wrong all this time. Sometimes I feel like going back there and talking to her one more time but then I get scared. I wonder if she is angry at me now. I don't know. So many years have passed. Maybe I was wrong, I don't know.

Would you go to see her if I asked you? She changed the promise once. She could do it again, don't you think? I don't want Maya to lose her sight. The pearls are great. They really helped us when I was struggling, I didn't know what to do and they solved our problems but we could do without them if it guaranteed that Maya would not lose her sight. I don't know what she will grow up to be but I don't want the sea to be her only option. She could be anything. She could want to live far away from the sea for whatever reason. If that's the case, why should she have to suffer? It is not fair, she hasn't made any promise to anyone. She is just a child. What do you think? Is it worth a try? It is, right? We should go. We should go and talk to Sila. Can I go? Would she come to the surface so I can talk to her too?

Hold on, calm down. That's a lot of questions. Let me think. Let me think about it, ok?

Leona thought about it. She thought about it and said nothing. She didn't speak much, maybe as a habit, as she had been living alone for a while now, or maybe because she didn't want to talk about what Ida wanted to do. She was going about her life, spending time in the garden with Maya, showing her how to take care of flowers, herbs and fruits. Maya followed her like a shadow and kept quiet around her until she got distracted and started chasing a butterfly or exploring near the river. This lasted a few days, until there was no sea water left in Maya's bottles. She started complaining about her eyes being itchy and Ida didn't want to see what would happen next.

Maya and I are leaving tomorrow morning. We can't stay here, you know that, right? You heard her complain about her eyes. We have no sea water left. We have to go. I understand you want to stay here and that's fine but I can't let Maya lose her sight and I need to talk to Sila myself. I can go by myself, you don't have to get involved.

You are not going by yourself. I am coming with you but we are not leaving tomorrow morning. We are leaving now. If we hurry, we will get there at sundown. Less people on the beach at night. We can then go without worrying about who is watching.

13

They packed and left. Ida's heart was pounding. She was the one who wanted to do this but her whole body was resisting the idea. She was sweating and breathing hard, wondering what she was doing there. Watching the sun go down as they approached the village. Leona had been able to see for a couple of hours only after using a little bit of Maya's sea water. She was blind again but she was walking with confidence, and fast. Ida remembered she had lived there for several years. Her feet were taking her to the sea like they had so many times before. When they reached the water, Ida stopped. She was terrified. Going to the sea with Maya was one thing. They never went anywhere far and, when Maya communicated with her friend in the water, it was always playful, just a playdate. Now, it was about going far down and talking to someone who had caused all of this, someone who might want company; and Ida was not like her mother and her daughter, she might end up like her father, drowning trying to follow someone who was not like her. « Because you see someone doing something, doesn't mean you should do it too. Always take a moment to think about what could happen before you do anything you have never done before. » That was the kind of thing Leona would tell her when she was still a child and now Leona wanted her to stop thinking and follow her under the sea.

She knows what she is doing. I trust her. Leona thought.

What are you doing? Let's go!

Leona already had water up to her waist, with Maya on her back, while Leona was barely getting her ankles wet.

I'm coming!

Ida took one step, then another. She was looking at Maya, who had now jumped into the water and was playing in her usual way, disappearing under the water and coming back up, giggling. When the water reached her neck, Ida stopped again, terrified. She was trying to take a huge breath before diving. She was taking huge breaths and not diving. Leona and Maya were not there anymore. She felt a hand holding her arms and had enough time to take only half a breath before she was pulled down. She thought it was Leona but, when she opened her eyes, she didn't see her. She didn't see anyone. She could still feel the hand on her arm, keeping her down and leading her further down but she could not see anyone holding her. After a while, she could see Leona holding Maya's hand. Both of them were waving at her with their free hands. They were sitting on the sand, at the bottom of the sea. They seemed to be in their natural element, but Ida was not. She was confused and scared. Suddenly, she thought about her breathing. She had not been able to take a full breath before being dragged there, and it took a moment to get there. She had to go back up before she got out of breath. She tried getting free from the hand that was holding her arms but she couldn't. She started panicking and felt another hand on her back stroking her like you would a scared child.

I have to keep at least one hand on you to help you out. As long as you stay with me, you won't need to go up for air. You don't have to worry at all.

Ida gave a better look in the direction where the voice came from but was still unable to see anything.

Ida, this is Sila, your great grand-mother, said Leona.

Ida tried looking more closely but saw no-one. She extended her arms and could feel nothing but water. She focused on the hand she could feel on her arm, tried to touch it and felt water, a bit different, like moving water. It was strange. Everything was strange. She was down under the water, deep down, for several minutes. She did not understand how she was not dead. She was terrified. She looked at Maya, who was now happily twirling around and Leona, who was sitting peacefully. She felt out of place and her anxiety was growing. She thought about all she had planned to say, about how brave and fearless she had thought you would be, but now, she was there and all she could think about was how unnatural it felt to her to be there. She wanted some air; she wanted the wind on her skin. She wanted the sky and the stars, the earth, dry soil under her feet. She thought of Freda, who died hating the sea. She didn't hate the sea, she was grateful for it and the gifts she had received but she was not like Leona and Maya who clearly felt comfortable there. She felt tired, very tired suddenly. Her eyes closed. She felt she was going back up. Her wish was being granted. On the surface, she was floating with her head out of the sea. She looked at the stars in the sky for a while and then closed her eyes again.

14

She woke up as she felt a hand on her arm. She touched the hand and felt it was a real hand, tangible, familiar, human, a man's hand, and another one. The two hands pulled her out of the water and on a small boat. She looked at the man and didn't know what to say. How do you explain why you were sleeping in the sea? So she said nothing and the man started talking.

Many years ago, I found a woman in the sea just like you. She was tired and didn't want to talk to me, just like you. I thought it was funny. You know, being a fisherman like me, it's many hours being alone. No-one to talk to, it gets lonely and monotonous. So when I saw her, I welcomed the surprise and wanted to know more about her, but it caused me heartbreak in the end. I don't regret anything though. That's just how I am. I would do it again. Hell, I am doing it again right now, with you. When I see someone who seems to be in trouble, I'm going to save them from drowning but I learned my lesson. If you don't want to say what you were doing there, that's fine. We can sail back to the beach in silence. Just try and avoid putting yourself in a dangerous situation. The currents are strong around here.

Ida nodded and gave him her back. It took them a while to reach the beach. Ida had not realised she had been so far away. She got out of the boat. She thanked him and walked away. She had no clue where she was going. She didn't want him to think she was some kind of vagabond with nowhere to go so she walked. She was hungry. After a few minutes she heard some voices and smelled some food. She joined a few customers waiting to be served. She had no money on her. She searched her pockets and found a pearl. When no-one else needed to be served and the cook was alone, she walked up to her and explained she didn't have any money but wanted to pay with the pearl. The cook looked at her suspiciously.

Who are you?

My name is Ida. I swear it's a real pearl, I am not lying.

I know it's a real pearl. I am asking you who your mother is and who is your grand-mother?

What? Why do you need to know? Will you accept my payment?

You are Leona's daughter, right? You look just like Freda.

You knew my mother and my grand-mother?

Sit down. What do you want to eat?

Ida presented the pearl to the cook.

I don't want this. Everything is free for you. Anything you want. Do you eat fruits only like your mother?

I used to but now I eat more things.

Get over here and help yourself. Take what you want.

Ida joined the cook behind the table that separated her from her customers and helped herself to fruits and cake, thinking about how she ate cake for breakfast with Maya when she sold the first pearls. She looked at the sea and sighed.

Are you Lola? She asked.

Yes, so your mama did not forget me. She told you about the time she spent here. Where is she now?

Ida pointed at the sea.

Of course. Lola said.

I don't know when she is coming back. And my daughter is there too. I couldn't stay with them. I am not like them.

I know, you're like Freda. She told me everything.

Lola sat near Ida to look at the sea until a new customer arrived. Ida sat there, waiting for Leona and Maya to come back. She sometimes stood up and walked up and down the beach. She sometimes would go to Lola's place for a few minutes but always came back to the beach, feeling like they could come back at any moment. Lola asked her so many times to come to her place to sleep at night but Ida felt they might come back during the night to draw less suspicion. So she stayed there at night, fighting sleep to make sure she didn't miss them. But they did not come back. Not the first night, not the first week, not the first month either.

For the first time, after a month of waiting, Ida considered the fact that they might not be coming back. Maybe they were gone for good. Maybe they couldn't resist the feeling of the water on their skin, singing in harmony with Sila. Sila had first wanted to leave because she was lonely. She wanted to be around people who were like her. Leona and Maya were like her. They were together now. Why would they want to come back here, where their skin itches and their eyes get weak?

Maybe they were so happy they had already fully forgotten about ordinary Ida. She knocked on Lola's door and accepted to spend the night. She laid on a bed with fresh sheets and slept all night. She woke up feeling guilty for a second and immediately remembered why she was there. They had forgotten her. Her own daughter and mother. They had forgotten her. Lola's house was not on the beach but close enough so Ida could hear the sound of the waves. She listened and thought about Freda, running to the mountain to get away from this sound. She was angry, but deep down, she could not completely believe that it was over. She didn't want to run away to the mountain nor any other place. They might come back after a year, like Sila first did - she thought. She convinced herself that was what it was going to take, one year. It had happened before, and that's what it was all about, same story repeating itself. She was Freda, Maya was Leona, who was Sila. Same people, same story.

It had to be one year. They would come back. She could feel the Freda in her growing. She was near the sea everyday, helping Lola with her cooking and selling meals to the fishermen. She was looking at the sea everyday and hating it more and more. She had not touched it since that day when she thought she was going to die. She had been lying on the surface, looking at the stars, thinking she would fall and drown at any moment. She had fallen asleep and dreamed she was dead. She dreamed she was sitting on firm ground with Freda. She had not introduced herself, she had said nothing but Ida had known instantly it was Freda. There had sat in silence, looking at the sea. Freda was throwing rocks at it and looked half sad, half angry. When Ida had taken a rock to throw it too, Freda had stopped her and put the rock back on the ground. She had started looking at the sea again and clapping rhythmically. Ida had listened for a while before realising she was clapping too, softly at first then louder and louder. The waves in the sea became agitated and she thought she could see someone. That's when she had been woken up by the fisherman, who pulled her out of there.

She had seen him again many times. He was getting his meal from Lola like many others; rather he was acting as if he was going to get his meal. He stood around as if he was waiting for his turn but he never came too close. He recognised Ida but never said anything. He would just stay somewhere in her field of view and nod when she looked at him. She would get his plate ready, place it next to her and wait for him to come and sit there in silence for a while. He'd always stay there until the last customer had left, then give her a discreet nod and go away. Ida nodded back and tried not to think about him, who she thought he was. She had a fair share of family worries with Maya and Leona being gone for more than a month now. It felt like ages and she wondered how she was going to endure several more months if it really had to take a year for them to come back. She was staying with Lola now, laying down at night, worried about falling asleep and missing them coming back at night. She still felt they would come back at night for more caution. She kept changing her mind about the one year timeframe. She was convincing herself and then doubting herself. Every other night, she would sneak out to look at the water, check if she could see anything. She couldn't see anything. She felt maybe it was like when she was in the water and could not see Sila. She could feel her but not see her. Maybe she could see nothing but they were there. She got closer to the water, wet her feet and stared. She could not see anything. She stuck her hands in the sea and heard someone calling her.

Hey! What are you doing? it's too late to go for a swim! Don't you remember what I told you about strong currents?

She turned around and saw him, the fisherman.

Well it's too late for walking around yelling at people too. What are you doing here?

I can't sleep.

Me neither and I am not going for a swim. I don't think I will be swimming anytime soon.

Really? Aren't you an excellent swimmer?

No, why do you think that?

You remind me of someone, that's something she used to say, and she was an excellent swimmer. You have to be a good one too, otherwise I would not have found you so far away last time.

I was with excellent swimmers but they left me.

Did they drown?

No, I don't think so. They just left me. I am not like them, I can't do what they can.

If you want my opinion, there is no excuse for leaving someone behind. These people did you wrong. You should move on instead of losing sleep over them.

And who are you losing sleep over? Are you moving on?

I know I should live what I preach but no, I have not moved on yet. I am on my way too but it's a slow process. I guess I am too slow to make up my mind. It has always been a problem of mine. Sometimes people want you to make an immediate decision or they leave you behind.

He sat down and she joined him.

You know who I am, right?

I think I do.

You are looking for your mother?

And my daughter.

So you don't have the swimming and pearl thing?

No, my daughter does.

Where is the father?

Taken by the sea, in a hurricane.

Sorry about that.

Thanks.

Aren't you angry at the sea? For taking your husband, your mother and your daughter.

I think they are coming back. I mean my daughter and my mother, not my husband.

It's been a while.

I know.

When your mother left, I thought she would come back. She never did.

She kind of did.

Not for me. She came back for the sea, not for me. Who can compete with the sea? I used to go out there, rowing extra hard, beating the sea up a little - he laughed *- I knew it was useless but it felt good.*

He took a rock and threw it into the water, and another one, another one. After the seventh rock, he stood up and clapped his hands to get rid of the sand. He looked Ida in the eyes and clapped rhythmically long after the last grain of sand had fallen to the ground. She started clapping too. He nodded and left.

15

She sat there and clapped until she felt hypnotised. She stood up and walked to the sea, still clapping. She walked until the water wet her feet, reached her ankles, her knees, her waist. When the water reached her shoulders, she remembered how scared she had been that night so she clapped louder and felt stronger. The water was up to her neck when a song came out of her and her feet started moving too. She took one more step, now without feeling fear. Fully immersed, she felt at peace. She kept on walking further away, until she felt tired. She sat down on the water, on a chair and it moved her faster, further, deeper. For one second, she thought about needing to breathe but stopped herself and focused on clapping louder. She sang and clapped herself back to peacefulness. She felt she was getting there before the waves stopped. She remembered the touch of Sila as she felt her hand on her arm. This time, she did not panic. She didn't think about how out of place she might be. All she wanted was to find her daughter and mother. She couldn't think about anything else, but she didn't know where to go. She looked around and couldn't see them. She decided to go but felt Sila holding her back.

Not this way.

Sila pulled her in the opposite direction and Ida let herself be led, floating behind the water movement Sila was creating. When they stopped, Ida looked around intensely. She could see nothing but water. Sila grabbed her by her shoulders and blew on each of her eyes one by one. Surprised, Ida closed them. When she opened them back, she could see the contours of a face in front of her. She could see Sila, a transparent face looking back at her. She could see her full silhouette and many others around. They were gathering around her to observe her with curiosity. She was the only one here not being like water, she was a curiosity, like they were to her. She looked at each one of them as they took turns to face her. Some shook her hand or touched her shoulder. Her ears popped and she could hear them discuss whether it was a good idea or not to let someone like her be there and know about them. Some thought it was dangerous, some thought she could be trusted because of her family. They were talking as if she could not hear them. At the mention of Leona's name, she interrupted them.

Where is she? Where is my mother? And my daughter, where are they?

The voices stopped all at once. Sila took her hand and led her further away. She heard a song and could not help but joining in the clapping and harmonising. She smiled as she saw little Maya dancing around Leona. She sang louder and Maya turned to her. Both Maya and Leona hugged her while finishing the song.

Where have you been? - Leona asked. *You were just behind us and at some point you were gone. Sila told us you could breathe as long as you stayed in physical contact with her so why did you go? What happened?*

What happened is that I panicked. I thought I was not like you and I couldn't trust I wouldn't drown. I had to go back up.

You seem to be breathing alright. You are not drowning and Sila is not even touching you. How did that happen?

She told her about dreaming of Freda and talking to the fisherman. She explained how she felt with the clapping and the singing. Then she came back to the fisherman. She said she liked him and Leona should talk to him sometime.

I am not going to talk to him - Leona said. *I am staying here. I want to stay here.*

Why?

You see how Sila made a promise when she left the first time?

Ida nodded.

Then she changed it by coming back here.

Ida nodded again.

I am doing the same. I am waiting to see Manman Dlo and ask to stay in exchange of Maya not having any need for the water anymore. I don't want her skin nor her eyes to feel uncomfortable anymore when she is away from the sea. I want her to be free from this. I will talk to Manman and make it all ok.

How do you know this will work?

This will have to. It's the best thing to do for Maya.

Is it? Is it the best thing for Maya to be away from her grand-mother? I travelled all the way here so she could meet you and spend time with you, now you are telling me you want to go away.

Don't you want her eyes to be fully healed?

I do, but I don't want you to go.

I am not going anywhere. I am here. Just like Sila. You can find us here anytime you want. You can even travel or move away. As long as you are near the sea, you can always call on us. Look at yourself, you even found a way to come all the way down here, by yourself, without any help.

My father helped me. You acted like he would not be interested in me if you had stayed but you see, he has been there. Everyday. He has helped me.

You are right. He has been there and he will always be there. When I left, I told Lola where I was going. I also told her why; so when he came to her, looking for me, she sat him down and talked to him. She felt he deserved to know so she told him, that I was expecting and where I was. He showed up one day, telling me that he was ready to accept that I was different and that he was ready to accept you too, no matter how different you might be. I told him I wanted to stay away from the sea, as a tribute to my mother. I was already losing my sight again and I know he had to picture his life in the mountain, with a blind woman and a baby, trying to learn a new trade, him who had been a fisherman his whole life. He stayed with me for a few days, watched me take care of my garden, talked for hours about what kind of work he could try to do; until he realised the sea was all he had ever known and all he had ever wanted. He could not imagine his life without it. He said he would go back and work during the week, come back for the weekend. That's the compromise we agreed on. And then he broke my heart a second time. He never came back. I don't know what happened. Maybe he changed his mind. Maybe he met someone else and forgot about me. I don't know.

He didn't, Sila intervened

He didn't forget about you. He started sailing at night and shaking the water with a paddle. He was looking for me. He was calling me and beating the water. At first, I decided to ignore him but he would not stop. I felt he would never stop so I decided to come up and see what he wanted. He had a long speech ready. He asked me to give you your eyes back, as if I had stolen them from you. He said he would do anything. He asked me what I wanted in exchange. I know that you explained things to him but he had no understanding of how things work. I kept telling him that I could not act on your eyes. I was not that powerful. I am not.. He heard me but did not believe me. He pleaded and pleaded all night. He talked so much. He was getting more and more upset but I was too. There was nothing I could do and he kept insisting. I decided to go and never answer him again, but he kept coming back. Night after night.. He never gave up. People around him started worrying about him. His friends came after him to force him to come back to the land many times but he kept coming back. They stole his boat and destroyed it; so he came back swimming. They brought him back to the shore every time, but he kept coming back. Until I heard a conversation between some fishermen talking about how his family came from the city and got him admitted to a house for people who had lost their minds. He did not last a week. They found him one morning, under the water, in a bathtub.

But I saw him.

I know.

It doesn't make sense.

Baby, we are under water right now. I am not moving my lips but you can hear me. You are not breathing any air but you are living. Not everything makes sense if you want to believe only what you have been used to exists. I am sorry about your father but you see, that's also why I decided to come back here. I am not meant to be up there, mingling with humans and trying to make them understand my difference. They always end up getting hurt. We all know it from personal

experience.

So what should we do now? Should we all stay here?

What do you want to do?

I don't know. I don't think I want to stay here. I don't think I

want to be around Manman Dlo. This is where it all started, all

this pain. Why? Why could she not save you and let you go?

Because she wanted to stay.

A beautiful, soft but powerful voice had just spoken. Ida

immediately knew who it was and felt terrified.

You don't have to be afraid of me. I have never hurt you. I

have sent you messages to let you know how you could come

here and talk to your family. I sent your grand-mother and your father to talk to you. I am glad you listened to them and decided to come here.

But I don't want to stay. I don't want Maya to stay. I don't think my mother should sacrifice herself and stay. Most of all, I don't think Sila wanted to stay in the first place.

I am not asking you to stay. Maya is a child, she should be with you, so if you want to go, she will go with you. Now Leona, you want to stay so you can change Sila's promise and Sila, you made a promise to me but now you don't want your children to keep it.

She placed her hand on Ida's shoulder.

I understand many stories have been told to you recently. You heard about Sila, Freda and Leona. Now I want you to hear from me directly. I remember all these years, decades, centuries of boats crossing the oceans. I remember the tears and the pain. I remember the bodies falling down the water. I remember those who were tired and wanted nothing to do with life anymore. There were others who still had hope and wanted to live. I rescued those. I gave them a new place to live, away from all the craziness going on on firm ground. I made no difference, touched them with life, led them to their new home and kept an eye on them. All of them, those who wanted life. Until one day, there was an exception, someone I wanted to treat differently. Someone special. She came with a rhythm and a song. She was gifted, still is and I wanted to enjoy this song longer so, instead of sending her to live with the others, I offered her to stay and she said yes. I thought at some point she'd want to go join the others but she asked to stay here. She seemed happy until she wasn't anymore. She started changing the song, singing to the sun. she didn't want to stay here anymore but she didn't want to join the other people who came from the boats. She wanted out. She wanted to be out of the water so she could see the sun, the sky and feel the wind on her skin. She came up with a promise. The promise seemed difficult to keep but she insisted she could do it. This is what she wanted so I agreed.

She left, fell in love and became unhappy so I took her back and offered to take her to the people who were exactly like her, born on firm ground but living in the water, people who would understand her and love her the way she was, but she said no. She wanted to be with Freda. She went back and, when she saw that Freda was making the same mistake she had made before, she decided to come back for good and ask me to change the promise. I agreed to forget about the daily obligation and offer gifts only when the song pleases me, if there was any song at all. I was surprised she didn't ask to change the sea craving part but I guess she wanted to have some visits sometimes.

Ida looked at Sila, who was avoiding her gaze as well as Leona's.

I liked the visits too, from you Leona and recently from little Maya too. I have always kept an eye on you, to make sure you don't lack anything. Of course, I couldn't help much when Freda and Leona decided to go up to the mountain but the river runs back to me you know. The river told me you were

doing ok up there. I love and protect who loves me back. I

want you to be happy, Sila. You and your family. This promise

you made such a long time ago, we can forget about it and I

am not asking for anything in exchange. The only thing I have

ever asked for was for you to keep the promise you decided

to make. You could have decided to make no promise and just

ask for what you wanted.

I have given you what you asked for, every time you asked.

Once again today, I will give you what you want.

All eyes were on Sila, who seemed to be hesitating. Her gaze

was travelling from Leona to Ida and back to Manman Dlo.

She knew what she wanted but she was scared. She thought

maybe Manman Dlo would disapprove. Maybe Leona, Ida

would disapprove. Maybe they were upset with her now that

they understood all of this could have been avoided if Sila

had not made that promise to begin with. She felt silly and

guilty. Most of all, she was scared of making the wrong

decision. Leona moved close to her and said:

Say it. Say what you want. I am sure you can make the right decision.

Finally, Sila said.

I want to stay here. Firm ground is not for me anymore. It was silly of me to think I could go and live a life as if I had not been here all this time. I want to stay here and meet my people.

What do you want for your children? Manman Dlo asked.

I want them to go back to firm ground. This is what they have known their whole lives. They have a life there, habits, occupations, friends. I want them to live a life without scrutiny. I want them to come to the water and think of me only when they want to, nothing in exchange, no special link to the water. I just hope they won't forget about me.

We won't. Ida said, holding Maya's hand.

The water moved and twirled, pushing them around until they reached the sand of the beach. They laid there, exhausted for a moment then stood up and looked around. It was the middle of the night, there was no-one there. Ida looked at where she had been sitting with her father, where he was always standing when she was working with Lola, where she had become accustomed to leaving a plate for him. He was not there. The full moon gave them all the light they needed to walk to Lola's house. Lola welcomed them inside and knew not to ask any questions when she saw how tired they looked.

16

Leona woke up first and went straight to the house she had been living in in her younger years, when she thought she could have a life in and out of the sea. She started pulling out bad weeds and checking what was salvageable in the garden. Ida joined her later and started cleaning the house while Maya went to the beach with Lola. When they came back, they found Leona and Ida, sitting in the garden, eating fruits and listening to the waves.

Maya made a friend today, Lola said. *The daughter of your neighbour. They played on the beach while we were working. It looks like they could become best friends, if you decide to stay.*

We are staying. Leona said.

Maya and Lola joined them on the bench where they would

sing songs and remember Manman Sila for the years to

come.

TABLE OF CONTENTS

Printed in Great Britain
by Amazon

19342652R00139